Sherwin Cody

Four Famous American Writers

Washington Irving, Edgar Allan Poe, James Russell Lowell, Bayard Taylor - a book

for young Americans

Sherwin Cody

Four Famous American Writers
Washington Irving, Edgar Allan Poe, James Russell Lowell, Bayard Taylor - a book for young Americans

ISBN/EAN: 9783337349509

Printed in Europe, USA, Canada, Australia, Japan

Cover: Foto ©Andreas Hilbeck / pixelio.de

More available books at **www.hansebooks.com**

FOUR
FAMOUS AMERICAN WRITERS

WASHINGTON IRVING
EDGAR ALLAN POE
JAMES RUSSELL LOWELL
BAYARD TAYLOR

A BOOK FOR YOUNG AMERICANS

BY

SHERWIN CODY
Author of "Four American Poets," etc., etc.

WERNER SCHOOL BOOK COMPANY

NEW YORK   CHICAGO   BOSTON

CONTENTS

THE STORY OF WASHINGTON IRVING

THE STORY OF EDGAR ALLAN POE

THE STORY OF JAMES RUSSELL LOWELL

THE STORY OF BAYARD TAYLOR

THE STORY OF
WASHINGTON IRVING

WASHINGTON IRVING.

WASHINGTON IRVING

CHAPTER I

HIS CHILDHOOD

The Revolutionary War was over. The British soldiers were preparing to embark on their ships and sail back over the ocean, and General Washington would soon enter New York city at the head of the American army. While all true patriots were rejoicing at this happy turn of affairs, a little boy was born who was destined to be the first great American author.

William Irving, the father of this little boy, had been a merchant in New York city. He had been very prosperous until the war broke out. After the battle of Long Island, the British then occupying the city, he had taken his family to New Jersey. But later, although he was a loyal American, he went back to the city to attend to his business. There he helped the American cause by doing everything he could for the American prisoners whom the British held. His wife, especially, had a happy way of persuading Sir Henry Clinton, and when the British general saw her coming, he prepared himself to grant any request about the prisoners which she might make. Often she sent them food from her own table, and cared for them when they were sick.

When their last son, the eleventh child, was born, on April 3, 1783, the parents showed their loyalty by naming him Washington, after the beloved Father of his Country.

Six years after this, George Washington was elected president, and went to New York to live. The Scotch maid who took care of little Washington Irving made up her mind to introduce the boy to his great namesake. So one day she followed the general into a shop, and, pointing to the lad, said, "Please, your honor, here's a bairn was named after you." Washington turned around, smiled, and placing his hand on the boy's head, gave him his blessing. Little did General Washington suspect that in later years this boy, grown to manhood and become famous, would write his biography.

In those days New York was only a small town at the south end of Manhattan Island. It extended barely as far north as the place where now stand the City Hall and the Postoffice. Broadway was then a country road. The Irvings lived at 131 William Street, afterward moving across to 128. This is now one of the oldest parts of New York. The streets in that section are narrow, and the buildings, though put up long after Irving's birth, seem very old.

Here the little boy grew up with his brothers and sisters. At four he went to school. His first teacher was a lady ; but he was soon transferred to a school kept by an old Revolutionary soldier who became so fond of the boy that he gave him the pet name of "General." This teacher liked him because, though often in mischief, he never tried to protect himself by telling a falsehood, but always confessed the truth.

Washington was not very fond of study, but he was a great reader. At eleven his favorite stories were "Robinson Crusoe" and "Sindbad the Sailor." Besides these, he read many books of travel, and soon found himself wishing that he might go to sea. As he grew up he was able to gratify his taste for travel, and some of his finest books and stories relate to his experiences in foreign lands. In the introduction to the "Sketch Book" he says, "How wistfully would I wander about the pier-heads in fine weather, and watch the parting ships bound to distant climes—with what longing eyes would I gaze after their lessening sails, and waft myself in imagination to the ends of the earth!"

CHAPTER II

IRVING'S FIRST VOYAGE UP THE HUDSON RIVER

Irving's first literary composition seems to have been a play written when he was thirteen. It was performed at the house of a friend, in the presence of a famous actress of that day; but in after years Irving had forgotten even the title.

His schooling was finished when he was sixteen.

His elder brothers had attended college, and he never knew exactly why he did not. But he was not fond of hard study or hard work. He lived in a sort of dreamy leisure, which seemed particularly suited to his light, airy genius, so full of humor, sunshine, and loving-kindness.

(After leaving school, he began to study law in the office of a certain Henry Masterton. This was in the year 1800. He was admitted to the bar six years later; but he spent a great deal more of the intervening time in traveling and scribbling than in the study of law. His first published writing was a series of letters signed "Jonathan Oldstyle," printed in his brother's daily paper, "The Morning Chronicle," when the writer was nineteen years old.

Irving's first journey was made the very year after he left school. It was a voyage in a sailing boat up the Hudson river to Albany; and a land journey from there to Johnstown, New York, to visit two married sisters. In the early days this was on the border of civilization, where the white traders went to buy furs from the Indians. Steamboats and railroads had not been invented, and a journey that can now be made in a few hours, then required several days. Years afterward, Irving described his first voyage up the Hudson.

"My first voyage up the Hudson," said he, "was made in early boyhood, in the good old times before steamboats and railroads had annihilated time and space, and driven all poetry and romance out of travel. . . . We enjoyed the beauties of the river in those days.*

"I was to make the voyage under the protection of a relative of mature age—one experienced in the river. His first care was to look out for a favorite sloop and captain, in which there was great choice. . . .

"A sloop was at length chosen; but she had yet to complete her freight and secure a sufficient number of passengers. Days were consumed in drumming up a cargo. This was a tormenting delay to me, who was about to make my first voyage, and who, boy-like, had packed my trunk

* Irving was the first to describe the wonderful beauties of the Hudson river.

on the first mention of the expedition. How often that trunk had to be unpacked and repacked before we sailed !

"At length the sloop actually got under way. As she worked slowly out of the dock into the stream, there was a great exchange of last words between friends on board and friends on shore, and much waving of handkerchiefs when the sloop was out of hearing.

" . . . What a time of intense delight was that first sail through the Highlands! I sat on the deck as we slowly tided along at the foot of those stern mountains, and gazed with wonder and admiration at cliffs impending far above me, crowned with forests, with eagles sailing and screaming around them ; or listened to the unseen stream dashing down precipices; or beheld rock, and tree, and cloud, and sky reflected in the glassy stream of the river. . . .

"But of all the scenery of the Hudson, the Kaatskill Mountains had the most witching effect on my boyish imagination. Never shall I forget the effect upon me of the first view of them predominating over a wide extent of country, part wild, woody, and rugged; part softened away into all the graces of cultivation. As we slowly floated along, I lay on the deck and watched them through a long summer's day, undergoing a thousand mutations under the magical effects of atmosphere; sometimes seeming to approach, at other times to recede; now almost melting into hazy distance, now burnished by the hazy sun, until, in the evening, they printed themselves against the glowing sky in the deep purple of an Italian landscape."

CHAPTER III

A TRIP TO MONTREAL

Soon after returning from this trip, Irving became a clerk in the law office of a Mr. Hoffman. There was a warm friendship between him and Mr. Hoffman's family. Mrs. Hoffman was his lifelong friend and, as he afterwards said, like a sister to him; and he finally fell in love with Matilda, one of Mr. Hoffman's daughters, and was engaged to be married to her. Her sad death at the age of seventeen was perhaps the greatest unhappiness of his life. He never married, but held her memory sacred as long as he lived.

In 1803 he was invited by Mr. Hoffman to go with him to Montreal and Quebec. Irving kept a journal during this expedition, and it shows what a rough time travelers had in those days.

Part of the way they sailed in a scow on Black River. They were partially sheltered from the rain by sheets stretched over hoops. At night they went ashore and slept in a log cabin.

One morning after a rainy night they awoke to find the sky clear and the sun shining brightly. Setting out again in their boat, they were soon surprised by meeting three canoes in pursuit of a deer.

"The deer made for our shore," says Irving in his journal. "We pushed ashore immediately, and as it passed, Mr. Ogden fired and wounded it. It had been wounded before. I threw off my coat and prepared to swim after it. As it came near, a man rushed through the bushes, sprang into the water, and made a grasp at the animal.

He missed his aim, and I jumped after, fell on his back, and sunk him under water. At the same time I caught the deer by one ear, and Mr. Ogden seized it by a leg. The submerged gentleman, who had risen above the water, got hold of another. We drew it ashore, when the man immediately dispatched it with a knife. We claimed a haunch for our share, permitting him to keep all the rest."

Irving had one or two experiences with the Indians which were not altogether pleasant at the time, but which afterward appeared very amusing.

On one occasion he went with another young man to a small island in a river, where he hoped to be able to hire a boat to take the party to a place some distance farther down the stream. They found there a wigwam in which were a number of Indians, both men and women; but the Indian they were looking for was away selling furs.

He soon came in, with his squaw, who was rather a pretty woman. Both he and she had been drinking. While the other young man was trying to explain their business, the Indian woman sat down beside Irving, and in her half drunken way began to pay him great attention.

The husband, a tall, strapping Hercules of an Indian, sat scowling at them with his blanket drawn up to his chin, and his face between his hands, while his elbows rested on his knees.

But soon the Indian could no longer endure the flirtation his wife was carrying on with Irving. He rushed upon him, calling him a "cursed Yankee," and gave him a blow which stretched him on the floor.

While Irving was picking himself up and getting out of the way, his friend went to the Indian and tried to quiet him. By this time the feelings of the drunken redman had quite changed. He fell on the young man's neck, exchanged names with him after the Indian fashion, and declared that they would be sworn friends and brothers as long as they lived.

Irving hastened to get into his boat, and he and his companion made off as quickly as possible, having no wish for any further intercourse with drunken Indians.

CHAPTER IV

IRVING GOES TO EUROPE

Irving's health was by no means good, and his friends were so alarmed that when he was twenty-one they planned a trip to Europe for him. As he stepped on board the boat that was to take him, the captain eyed him from head to foot and remarked to himself, "There's a chap who will go overboard before we get across."

To the surprise of the captain and other passengers, however, he did not die, but got much better.

He disembarked at Bordeaux, in France, and joining a merry company, traveled with them in a kind of stagecoach called a diligence.

Among the company were a jolly little Pennsylvania doctor, and a French officer going home to see his mother. In one of the little French towns where they stopped they had an amusing experience, which Irving has described in his journal.

"In one of our strolls in the town of Tonneins," says he, "we entered a house where a number of girls were quilting. They gave me a needle and set me to work. My bad French seemed to give them much amusement. They asked me several questions; as I could not understand them I made them any answer that came into my head, which caused a great deal of laughter amongst them.

"At last the little doctor told them that I was an English prisoner, whom the young French officer (who was with us) had in custody. Their merriment immediately gave place to pity.

" 'Ah, the poor fellow!' said one to another, 'he is merry, however, in all his trouble.'

" 'And what will they do with him?' said a young woman to the traveler.

" 'Oh, nothing of consequence,' replied he; 'perhaps shoot him or cut off his head.'

"The honest souls seemed quite distressed for me, and when I mentioned that I was thirsty, a bottle of wine was immediately placed before me, nor could I prevail on them to take a recompense. In short, I departed, loaded with their good wishes and benedictions, and I suppose I furnished a theme of conversation throughout the village."

Years afterward, when Mr. Irving was minister

to Spain, he went some miles out of his way to visit this town. Says he:

"As my carriage rattled through the quiet streets of Tonneins, and the postilion smacked his whip with the French love of racket, I looked out for the house where, forty years before, I had seen the quilting party. I believe I recognized the house; and I saw two or three old women, who might once have formed part of the merry group of girls; but I doubt whether they recognized in the stout, elderly gentleman, who thus rattled in his carriage through their streets, the pale young English prisoner of forty years since."

In this manner he wandered about for nearly two years. He visited Genoa, the birthplace of Columbus, and climbed Mount Vesuvius. He dined with Madame de Stael, the famous author of "Corinne." At Rome he met Washington Allston, the great American painter, then a young man not much older than he. They became good friends, and Allston afterward illustrated some of Irving's works. Irving was tempted to remain in

Rome and become a painter like Allston. But he finally decided that he did not have any special talent for art, and went home to finish his study of law.

CHAPTER V

"SALMAGUNDI"

Washington Irving returned to New York, quite restored to health; and there he soon became a social hero. Trips to Europe were so uncommon in those days that to have made one was a distinction in itself. Besides, Irving was now a polished young gentleman, very fond of amusement; and having become a lawyer with little to do, he made up his mind to enjoy himself.

He and his brother Peter, with a number of young men about the same age, called themselves "the nine worthies," or the "lads of Kilkenny," and many a gay time they had together,—rather too gay, some people thought. One of their favorite resorts was an old family mansion, which had descended from a deceased uncle to one of the nine lads. It was on the banks of the Passaic river, about a mile from Newark, New Jersey. It was full of antique furniture, and the walls were adorned with old family portraits. The place was in charge of an old man and his wife and a negro boy, who were the sole occupants, except when the nine would sally forth from New York and enliven its solitudes with their madcap pranks and orgies.

"Who would have thought," said Irving at the age of sixty-three to another of those nine lads, "that we should ever have lived to be two such respectable old gentlemen!"

About this time Irving and a friend named James K. Paulding proposed to start a paper, to be called "Salmagundi." It was an imitation of Addison's *Spectator*, and consisted of light, humorous essays, most of them making fun of the fads and fancies of New York life in those days. The numbers were published from a week to a month apart, and were continued for about a year.

The young men had no idea of making money by the venture, for they were then well-to-do; but to their surprise it proved a great success, and the publisher is said to have made ten or fifteen thousand dollars out of it. He afterwards paid the editors four hundred dollars each.

Irving now visited Philadelphia, Boston, and other places. He thought of trying for a government office, and was tempted into politics. His description of his experience is amusing enough.

"Before the third day was expired, I was as deep in mud and politics as ever a moderate gentleman would wish to be; and I drank beer with the multitude; and I talked handbill-fashion with the demagogues, and I shook hands with the mob—whom my heart abhorreth. 'Tis true, for the two first days I maintained my coolness and indifference. . . . But the third day—ah! then came the tug of war. My patriotism all at once blazed forth, and I determined to save my country! O, my friend, I have been in such holes and corners; such filthy nooks, sweep offices, and oyster cellars!"

He closes by saying that this saving one's country is such a sickening business that he wants no more of it.

CHAPTER VI

"DIEDRICH KNICKERBOCKER"

On October 26, 1809, there appeared in the *New York Evening Post* the following paragraph:

"DISTRESSING.

"Left his lodgings, some time since, and has not since been heard of, a small elderly gentleman, dressed in an old black coat and cocked hat, by the name of Knickerbocker. As there are some reasons for believing he is not entirely in his right mind, and as great anxiety is entertained about him, any information concerning him left either at the Columbian Hotel, Mulberry street, or at the office of this paper, will be thankfully received.

"P.S. Printers of newspapers will be aiding the cause of humanity in giving an insertion to the above."

Two weeks later a letter was printed in the *Evening Post*, signed "A Traveler," saying that such a gentleman as the one described had been seen a little above King's Bridge, north of New York, "resting himself by the side of the road."

Ten days after this the following letter was printed:

"*To the Editor of the Evening Post:*

"Sir,—You have been good enough to publish in your paper a paragraph about Mr. Diedrich Knickerbocker, who was missing so strangely some time since; but a very curious kind of a written book has been found in his room, in his own handwriting. Now I wish to notice* him, if he is still alive, that if he does not return and pay off his bill for boarding and lodging, I shall have to dispose of his book to satisfy me for the same.

"I am, sir, your obedient servant,
"Seth Handaside,
"Landlord of the Independent Columbian Hotel, Mulberry Street."

On November 28th there appeared in the advertising columns the announcement of "A History of New York," in two volumes, price three dollars.

---

* Legal term, meaning "to give notice to."

The advertisement says, "This work was found in the chamber of Mr. Diedrich Knickerbocker, the old gentleman whose sudden and mysterious disappearance has been noticed. It is published in order to discharge certain debts he has left behind."

When the book was published the people took it up, expecting to find a grave and learned history of New York. It was dedicated to the New York Historical Society, and began with an account of the supposed author, Mr. Diedrich Knickerbocker. "He was a small, brisk-looking old gentleman, dressed in a rusty black coat, a pair of olive velvet breeches, and a small cocked hat. He had a few gray hairs plaited and clubbed behind. . . . The only piece of finery which he bore about him was a bright pair of square silver shoe-buckles." The landlord of the inn, who writes this description, adds: "My wife at once set him down for some eminent country schoolmaster."

Imagine for yourself the astonishment, and then the amusement—in some cases even the anger—of those who read, to find a most ludicrous description of the old Dutch settlers of New York, the ancestors of the most aristocratic families of the metropolis of America. The people that laughed got the best of it, however, and the book was considered one of the popular successes of the day.

The real author of this book was, of course, Washington Irving. When forty years later the book was to be included in his collected works he wrote an "Apology," in which he says, " When I find, after a lapse of nearly forty years, this haphazard production of my youth still cherished among them (the New Yorkers); when I find its very name become a 'household word,' and used to give the home stamp to everything recommended for popular acceptance, such as Knickerbocker societies, Knickerbocker insurance companies, Knickerbocker steamboats, Knickerbocker omnibuses, Knickerbocker bread, and Knickerbocker ice,—and when I find New Yorkers of Dutch descent priding themselves upon being 'genuine Knickerbockers,' I please myself with the persuasion that I have struck the right chord."

CHAPTER VII

A COMIC HISTORY OF NEW YORK

"Knickerbocker's History of New York" was undertaken by Irving and his brother Peter as a parody on a book that had lately appeared, entitled "A Picture of New York." The two young men, one of whom had already proved himself something of an author, were so full of humor and the spirit of mischief that they must amuse themselves and their friends, and they thought this a good way of doing it. There was to be an introduction giving the history of New York from the foundation of the world, and the main body of the book was to consist of "notices of the customs, manners, and institutions of the city; written in a serio-comic vein, and treating local errors, follies, and abuses with good-humored satire."

The introduction was not more than fairly begun when Peter Irving started for Europe, leaving the completion of the work to the younger brother. Washington decided to change the plan, and merely give a humorous history of the Dutch settlement of New York.

Let us take a peep into this amusing history. First, here is the portrait of "that worthy and irrecoverable discoverer (as he has justly been called), Master Henry Hudson," who "set sail from Holland in a stout vessel called the Half-Moon, being employed by the Dutch East India Company to seek a northwest passage to China."

"Henry (or as the Dutch historians call him, Hendrick) Hudson was a seafaring man of renown, who had learned to smoke tobacco under Sir Walter Raleigh, and is said to have been the first to introduce it into Holland, which gained him much popularity in that country, and caused him to find great favor in the eyes of their High Mightinesses, the Lords States General, and also of the honorable East India Company. He was a short, square, brawny old gentleman, with a double chin, a mastiff mouth, and a broad copper nose, which was supposed in those days to have acquired its fiery hue from the constant neighborhood of his tobacco pipe.

"He wore a commodore's cocked hat on one side of his head. He was remarkable for always jerking up his breeches when he gave out his orders, and his voice sounded not unlike the brattling of a tin trumpet—owing to the number of hard northwesters which he had swallowed in the course of his seafaring.

"Such was Hendrick Hudson, of whom we have heard so much and know so little."

You must read in the history itself the amusing account of Ten Breeches and Tough Breeches. One of the Dutch colonists bought of the Indians for sixty guelders as much land as could be covered by a man's breeches. When the time for measuring came Mr. Ten Breeches was produced, and peeling off one pair of breeches after another, soon produced enough material to surround the entire island of Manhattan, which was thus bought for sixty guelders, or Dutch dollars.

In due time came the first Dutch governor, Wouter Van Twiller.

Governor Van Twiller was five feet six inches in height, and six feet five inches in circumference, his figure "the very model of majesty and lordly grandeur." On the very morning after he had entered upon his office, he gave an example of his great legal knowledge and wise judgment.

As the governor sat at breakfast an important old burgher came in to complain that Barent Bleecker refused to settle accounts, which was very annoying, as there was a heavy balance in the complainant's favor. "Governor Van Twiller, as I have already observed, was a man of few words; he was likewise a mortal enemy to multiplying writings—or being disturbed at his breakfast. Having listened attentively to the statement of Wandle Schoonhoven, giving an occasional grunt, as he shoveled a spoonful of Indian pudding into his mouth,—either as a sign that he relished the dish or comprehended the story,—he called unto him his constable, and pulling out of his breeches pocket a huge jack-knife, dispatched it after the defendant as a summons, accompanied by his to-bacco-box as a warrant."

When the account books were before him, "the sage Wouter took them one after the other, and having poised them in his hands, and attentively counted over the number of leaves, fell straightway into a great doubt, and smoked for half an hour without saying a word; at length, laying his finger beside his nose, and shutting his eyes for a moment, with the air of a man who had just caught a subtle idea by the tail, he slowly took his pipe from his mouth, puffed forth a column of tobacco smoke, and with marvelous gravity and solemnity pronounced, that, having carefully counted over the leaves and weighed the books, it was found that one was just as thick and heavy as the other; therefore, it was the final opinion of the court that the accounts were equally balanced; therefore, Wandle should give Barent a receipt, and Barent should give Wandle a receipt, and the constable should pay the costs."

It is not wonderful that this was the first and last lawsuit during his administration, and that no one was found who cared to hold the office of constable.

This is only one of scores of droll stories to be found in this most interesting "history."

CHAPTER VIII

FIVE UNEVENTFUL YEARS

It seems strange that the success of the "History of New York" did not make Irving a professional man of letters at once. The profits on the first edition were three thousand dollars, and several other editions were to follow steadily. But though he wished to be a literary man, and now knew that he might make a fair living by his writings, there was still lacking the force to compel him to work. He had always lived in easy circumstances, doing as he liked, enjoying society, and amusing himself, and it was hard for him to devote his attention strictly to any set task.

He applied for a clerkship at Albany, but failed to get it. Then his brothers, with whom he must have been a great favorite, as he was the youngest of the family, arranged a mercantile business in which he was to be a partner. Peter was to buy goods in England and ship them to New York, while Ebenezer was to sell them. Washington was to be a silent partner, and enjoy one fifth of the profits. At first he objected to taking no active part in the business; but his brothers persuaded him that this was his chance to become independent and have his entire time for literary work.

But five years passed away and little was accomplished. This covered the period of the War of 1812. At first Irving was opposed to the war; but when he heard the news of the burning of Washington his patriotism blazed forth. "He was descending the Hudson in the steamboat when the tidings first reached him," says his nephew in the biography which he wrote. "It was night and the passengers had betaken themselves to their settees to rest, when a person came on board at Poughkeepsie with the news of the inglorious triumph, and proceeded in the darkness of the cabin to relate the particulars: the destruction of the president's house, the treasury, war, and navy offices, the capitol, the depository of the national library and the public records. There was a momentary pause after the speaker had ceased, when some paltry spirit lifted his head from his settee, and in a tone of complacent derision, 'wondered what *Jimmy* Madison would say now.' 'Sir,' said Mr. Irving, glad of an escape to his swelling indignation, 'do you seize on such a disaster only for a sneer? Let me tell you, sir, it is not now a question about *Jimmy* Madison or *Jimmy* Armstrong.* The pride and honor of the nation are wounded; the country is insulted and disgraced by this barbarous success, and every loyal citizen should feel the ignominy and be earnest to avenge it.' 'I could not see the fellow,' said Mr. Irving when he related the anecdote, 'but I let fly at him in the dark.'"

As soon as he reached New York, Irving went to the governor and offered his services. He was immediately appointed military secretary and aide with the rank of colonel. His duties were neither difficult nor dangerous, and he enjoyed his position; but he was glad when the war came to an end the following year.

When the War of 1812 was over, his friend

* The Secretary of War.

Commodore Decatur invited him to accompany him on an expedition to the Mediterranean, the United States having declared war against the pirates of Algiers. Irving's trunks were put on board the *Guerriere*, but as the expedition was delayed on account of the escape of Napoleon from Elba, he had them again brought ashore, and finally gave up his plan of going with Decatur. His mind was set on visiting Europe, however, and he immediately took passage for Liverpool in another vessel. Little did he think that he was not to return for seventeen years.

One of Irving's married sisters was living in Birmingham, and his brother Peter was in Liverpool managing the business in which he was a partner. Soon after Washington's arrival, however, Peter fell ill, and the younger brother was obliged to take charge of affairs. He found a great many bills to pay, and very little money with which to pay them. He was now beginning to face some of the stern realities of life. He worked hard; but the black cloud of ruin came nearer and nearer. Other difficulties were added to those they already had to face, and finally, in 1818, the brothers were obliged to go into bankruptcy.

It was now absolutely necessary that Irving should earn his living in some way. His brothers procured him an appointment at Washington; but to their astonishment he declined it and said he had made up his mind to live by his pen.

He immediately went to London and set to work on the "Sketch Book," and during the next dozen years wrote the greater number of his more famous works.

CHAPTER IX

FRIENDSHIP WITH SIR WALTER SCOTT

While he was worrying over the failure of his business, Irving was fortunate enough to make some distinguished literary friendships. He had already helped to introduce Thomas Campbell's works in the United States, and had written a biography of Campbell; one of the first things he did, therefore, after reaching Liverpool, was to go to see the English poet.

It was not until a little later that he became acquainted with Sir Walter Scott, who was the literary giant of those times. In 1813 Henry Brevoort, one of Irving's most intimate boyhood friends, had presented to Scott a copy of the "History of New York," and Scott had written a letter of thanks in which he said, "I have been employed these few evenings in reading the annals of Diedrich Knickerbocker aloud to Mrs. S. and two ladies who are our guests, and our sides have been absolutely sore with laughing. I think, too, there are passages which indicate that the author possesses powers of a different kind."

Irving, too, had been a great admirer of Scott's "Lady of the Lake." Campbell gave him a letter of introduction to the bard, and in a letter to his brother, Irving gives a delightful description of his visit to Abbotsford, Scott's home.

"On Saturday morning early," says he, "I took a chaise for Melrose; and on the way stopped at the gate of Abbotsford, and sent in my letter of introduction, with a request to know whether it would be agreeable for Mr. Scott to receive a visit from me in the course of the day. The glorious old minstrel himself came limping to the gate, and took me by the hand in a way that made me feel as if we were old friends; in a moment I was seated at his hospitable board among his charming little family, and here I have been ever since. . . . I cannot tell you how truly I have enjoyed the hours I have passed here. They fly by too quickly, yet each is loaded with story, incident, or song; and when I consider the world of ideas, images, and impressions that have been crowded upon my mind since I have been here, it seems incredible that I should only have been two days at Abbotsford."

And here is Scott's impression of Irving: "When you see Tom Campbell," he writes to a friend, "tell him, with my best love, that I have to thank him for making me known to Mr. Washington Irving, who is one of the best and pleasantest acquaintances I have made this many a day."

When the "Sketch Book" was coming out in the United States, and Irving was thinking of publishing it in England, he received some advice

and assistance from Scott; and finally Scott persuaded the great English publisher Murray to take
it up, even after that publisher had once declined
it. On this occasion Irving wrote to a friend as
follows:

"He (Scott) is a man that, if you knew, you
would love; a right honest-hearted, generous-
spirited being; without vanity, affectation, or
assumption of any kind. He enters into every
passing scene or passing pleasure with the interest
and simple enjoyment of a child.

CHAPTER X

"RIP VAN WINKLE"

Irving's most famous work is undoubtedly the
"Sketch Book"; and of the thirty-two stories and
essays in this volume, all Americans love best
"The Legend of Sleepy Hollow" and "Rip Van
Winkle."

After the failure of his business, when Irving
saw that he must write something at once to meet
his ordinary living expenses, he went up to Lon-

don and prepared several sketches, which he sent to his friend, Henry Brevoort, in New York. Among them was the story of Rip Van Winkle. This, with the other sketches, was printed in handsome form as the first number of a periodical, which was offered for sale at seventy-five cents. Though "The Sketch Book," as the periodical was called, professed to be edited by "Geoffrey Crayon, Gent.," every one knew that Washington Irving was the real author. In fact, the best story in the first number, "Rip Van Winkle," was represented to be a posthumous writing of Diedrich Knickerbocker, the author of the "History of New York."

There are few Americans who do not know the story of "Rip Van Winkle" by heart; for those who have not read the story, have at least seen the play in which Joseph Jefferson, the great actor, has made himself so famous.

Attached to the story is a note supposed to have been written by Diedrich Knickerbocker, which a careless reader might overlook, but which is an excellent introduction to the story. Says he:

"The story of Rip Van Winkle may seem incredible to many, but nevertheless I give it my full belief, for I know the vicinity of our old Dutch settlements to have been very subject to marvelous events and appearances. Indeed, I have heard many stranger stories than this in the villages along the Hudson; all of which were too well authenticated to admit of a doubt. I have even talked with Rip Van Winkle myself, who, when I last saw him, was a very venerable old man, and so perfectly rational and consistent on every point, that I think no conscientious person could refuse to take this into the bargain; nay, I have seen a certificate on the subject, taken before a country justice, and signed with a cross, in the justice's own handwriting. The story, therefore, is beyond the possibility of doubt."

Rip was truly an original character. He had a shrewish wife who was always scolding him; and he seems to have deserved all the cross things she said to him, for he had ''an insuperable aversion to all kinds of profitable labor—in other words, he was as lazy a fellow as you could find in all the country side."

Nevertheless, every one liked him, he was so good-natured. "He was a great favorite among all the good wives of the village, who took his part in all the family squabbles; and never failed whenever they talked those matters over in their evening gossipings, to lay all the blame on Dame Van Winkle. The children of the village, too, would shout with joy whenever he approached. He assisted at their sports, made their playthings, taught them to fly kites and shoot marbles, and told them long stories of ghosts, witches, and Indians. Whenever he went dodging about the village, he was surrounded by a troop of them, hanging on his skirts, clambering on his back, and playing a thousand tricks on him with impunity; and not a dog would bark at him throughout the neighborhood."

You can't find much fault with a man who is so well liked that even the dogs will not bark at him. You are reminded of Irving himself, who for so many years was so idle; and yet who, out of his very idleness, produced such charming stories.

"Rip Van Winkle," continues the narrative,

"was one of those happy mortals, of foolish, well-oiled dispositions, who take the world easy, eat white bread or brown, whichever can be got with least thought or trouble, and would rather starve on a penny than work for a pound. If left to himself, he would have whistled life away in perfect contentment; but his wife kept continually dinning in his ears about his idleness, his carelessness, and the ruin he was bringing on his family."

This description is as perfect and as delightful as any in the English language. Any one who cannot enjoy this has no perception of human nature, and no love of humor in his composition. In time Rip discovered that his only escape from his termagant wife was to take his gun, and stroll off into the woods with his dog. "Here he would sometimes seat himself at the foot of a tree, and share the contents of his wallet with Wolf, with whom he sympathized as a fellow sufferer in persecution. 'Poor Wolf,' he would say, 'thy mistress leads thee a dog's life of it; but never mind, my lad, whilst I live thou shalt never want a friend to stand by thee!' Wolf would wag his tail, look wistfully into his master's face, and if dogs can feel pity, I verily believe he reciprocated with all his heart."

Rip is just the sort of fellow to have some sort of adventure, and we are not at all astonished when we find him helping the dwarf carry his keg of liquor up the mountain. The description of "the odd-looking personages playing at nine-pins" whom he finds on entering the amphitheater, is a perfect picture in words; for the truly great writer is a painter of pictures quite as much as the great artist.

"They were dressed in a quaint outlandish fashion; some wore short doublets, others jerkins, with long knives in their belts. Their visages, too, were peculiar: one had a large head, broad face, and small piggish eyes; the face of another seemed to consist entirely of nose, and was surmounted by a white sugar-loaf hat, set off with a little red cock's tail. They all had beards of various shapes and colors. There was one who seemed to be the commander. He was a stout old gentleman, with a weather-beaten countenance; he wore a laced doublet, broad belt and hanger, high-crowned hat and feather, red stockings, and high-heeled shoes, with roses in them. . . . What seemed particularly odd to Rip was, that though these folks were evidently amusing themselves, yet they maintained the gravest faces, the most mysterious silence, and were, withal, the most melancholy party of pleasure he had ever witnessed. Nothing interrupted the stillness of the scene but the noise of the balls, which, whenever they were rolled, echoed along the mountains like rumbling peals of thunder."

But now comes a surprise. Rip indulges too freely in the contents of the keg and falls asleep. When he wakes he finds a rusty old gun beside him, and he whistles in vain for his dog. He goes back to the village; but everything and everybody is strange and changed. Putting his hand to his chin he finds that his beard has grown a foot. He has been sleeping twenty years.

But you must read the story for yourselves. It will bear reading many times, and each time you will find in it something to smile at and enjoy.

CHAPTER XI

LITERARY SUCCESS IN ENGLAND

"The Legend of Sleepy Hollow" also purports to be written by Diedrich Knickerbocker, and it is only less famous than "Rip Van Winkle." When he was a boy, Irving had gone hunting in Sleepy Hollow, which is not far from New York city; and in the latter part of his life he bought a low stone house there of Mr. Van Tassel and fitted it up for his bachelor home.

"The outline of this story," says his nephew Pierre Irving, "had been sketched more than a year before* at Birmingham, after a conversation with his brother-in-law, Van Wart, who had been dwelling on some recollections of his early years at Tarrytown, and had touched upon a waggish fiction of one Brom Bones, a wild blade, who professed to fear nothing, and boasted of his having once met the devil on a return from a nocturnal frolic, and run a race with him for a bowl of milk punch. The imagination of the author suddenly

---

* That is, before it was finally written and published.

kindled over the recital, and in a few hours he had scribbled off the framework of his renowned story, and was reading it to his sister and her husband. He then threw it by until he went up to London, where it was expanded into the present legend."

No sooner had the first number of the "Sketch Book," as published in New York, come to England, than a periodical began reprinting it, and Irving heard that a publisher intended to bring it out in book form. That made him decide to publish it in England himself, and he did so at his own expense. The publisher soon failed, and by Scott's help, as already explained, Irving got his book into the hands of Murray. Murray finally gave him a thousand dollars for the copyright. But when it was published, it proved so very popular that Murray paid him five hundred more. From that time forward he received large sums for his writings, both in the United States and in England.

The "Sketch Book" was followed by "Bracebridge Hall," consisting of stories and sketches of the same character; and later by the "Tales of a Traveller."

In the "Tales of a Traveller" we are most interested in "Buckthorne and his Friends," a series of English stories, with descriptions of literary life in London. Most famous of all is the account of a publishers' dinner, with a description of the carving partner sitting gravely at one end, with never a smile on his face, while at the other end of the table sits the laughing partner; and the poor authors are arranged at the table and are treated by the partners according to the number of editions their books have sold.

Irving's father was a Scotchman, and his mother was an Englishwoman; and one of his sisters and one of his brothers, as we have already learned, lived in England for many years. It is not strange, then, that England became to him a second home, and that many of his best stories and descriptions in the "Sketch Book," "Bracebridge Hall," and the "Tales of a Traveller" relate to English characters and scenes.

CHAPTER XII

IRVING GOES TO SPAIN

When Irving went to Liverpool in 1815, it was his intention to travel on the continent of Europe. As we have seen, business reasons made that impossible. But after the publication and success of the "Sketch Book" he was free. He was now certain of an income, and his reputation was so great that he attracted notice wherever he went.

In 1820, after having spent five years in England, he at last set out on his European journey. We cannot follow him in all his wanderings; but one country that he visited furnished him the materials for the most serious, and in one way the most important part of his literary work. This was Spain. Here he spent a great deal of time, returning again and again; and finally he was appointed United States minister to that country.

He first went to Spain to collect materials for the "Life and Voyages of Christopher Columbus." This was a much more serious work than anything he had before undertaken. It was, unlike the history of New York, a genuine investigation of facts derived from the musty old volumes of the libraries of Spanish monasteries and other ancient collections. It was a record of the life of the discoverer of America that was destined to remain the highest authority on that subject. Murray, the London publisher, paid him over fifteen thousand dollars for the English copyright alone.

In his study among the ruins of Spain, Irving found many other things which greatly interested him—legends, and tales of the Moors who had once ruled there, and of the ruined beauties of the Moorish palace of the Alhambra. His imagination was set on fire, he was delighted with the images of by-gone days of glittering pageantry which his fancy called up. Before his history of Columbus was finished, he began the writing of a book so precisely to his taste that he could not restrain himself until it was finished. This was the "Chronicle of the Conquest of Granada"—a true history, but one which reads more like a romance of the Middle Ages than a simple record of facts.

This was followed by four other books based on Spanish history and legend. It seemed as if Irving could never quite abandon this entrancing subject, for during the entire remainder of his life he went back to it constantly.

When his great history of the life of Columbus was published and proved its merit, Irving was honored in a way he had little expected in his more idle days. The Royal Society of Literature bestowed upon him one of two fifty-guinea* gold medals awarded annually, and the University of Oxford conferred the degree of LL. D.

The "Life of Columbus" was followed in 1831 by the "Voyages of the Companions of Columbus." In the following year Irving returned to the United States after an absence of seventeen years.

He was no longer an idle young man unable to fix his mind on any serious work; he had become the most famous of American men of letters. When he reached New York his countrymen hastened to heap honors upon him, and almost overwhelmed him with public attentions.

---

* Two hundred and fifty dollars.

CHAPTER XIII

"THE ALHAMBRA"

Just before Irving's return to the United States in 1832, he prepared for publication some sketches which he had made three or four years before while living for a few months in the ruins of the Alhambra, the ancient palace of the Moorish kings when they ruled the kingdom of Granada. Next to the stories of "Rip Van Winkle" and the "Legend of Sleepy Hollow," nothing that Irving has written has proved more popular than this volume of "The Alhambra;" and it has made the ancient ruin a place of pilgrimage for tourists in Europe ever since.

In this volume Irving not only describes in his own peculiarly charming manner his experiences in the halls of the Alhambra itself, but he gives many of the stories and legends of the place, most of which were told to him by Mateo Ximenes, a "son of the Alhambra," who acted as his guide. This is the way he came to secure Mateo's services:

"At the gate were two or three ragged, superannuated soldiers, dozing on a stone bench, the successors of the Zegris and the Abencerrages; while a tall, meagre valet, whose rusty-brown cloak was evidently intended to conceal the ragged state of his nether garments, was lounging in the sunshine and gossipping with the ancient sentinel on duty. He joined us as we entered the gate, and offered his services to show us the fortress.

"I have a traveler's dislike to officious ciceroni, and did not altogether like the garb of the applicant.

"'You are well acquainted with the place, I presume?'

"'Nobody better; in fact, sir, I am a son of the Alhambra.'

"The common Spaniards have certainly a most poetical way of expressing themselves. 'A son of the Alhambra!' the appellation caught me at once; the very tattered garb of my new acquaintance assumed a dignity in my eyes. It was emblematic of the fortunes of the place, and befitted the progeny of a ruin."

Accompanied by Mateo, the travelers pass on to

"the great vestibule, or porch of the gate," which "is formed by an immense Arabian arch, of the horseshoe form, which springs to half the height of the tower. On the keystone of this arch, is engraven a gigantic hand. Within the vestibule, on the keystone of the portal, is sculptured, in like manner, a gigantic key," emblems, say the learned, of Moorish superstition and religious belief.

"A different explanation of these emblems, however, was given by the legitimate son of Alhambra, and one more in unison with the notions of the common people, who attach something of mystery and magic to everything Moorish, and have all kinds of superstitions connected with this old Moslem fortress. According to Mateo, it was a tradition handed down from the oldest inhabitants, and which he had from his father and grandfather, that the hand and key were magical devices on which the fate of the Alhambra depended. The Moorish king who built it was a great magician, or, as some believed, had sold himself to the devil, and had laid the whole fortress under a magic spell. By this means it had remained standing for several years, in defiance of storms and earthquakes, while almost all other buildings of the Moors had fallen to ruin and disappeared. This spell, the tradition went on to say, would last until the hand on the outer arch should reach down and grasp the key, when the whole pile would tumble to pieces, and all the treasures buried beneath it by the Moors would be revealed."

The travelers at once made application to the governor for permission to take up their residence in the palace of the Alhambra, and to their astonishment and delight he placed his own suite of apartments at their disposal, as he himself preferred to live in the city of Granada.

Irving's companion soon left him, and he remained sole lord of the palace. For a time he occupied the governor's rooms, which were very scantily furnished; but one day he came upon an eerie suite of rooms which he liked better. They were the rooms that had been fitted up for the beautiful Elizabetta of Farnese, the second wife of Philip V.

"The windows, dismantled and open to the wind and weather, looked into a charming little secluded garden, where an alabaster fountain sparkled among roses and myrtles, and was surrounded by orange and citron trees, some of which flung their branches into the chambers." This was the garden of Lindaraxa.

"Four centuries had elapsed since the fair Lindaraxa passed away, yet how much of the fragile beauty of the scenes she inhabited remained! The garden still bloomed in which she delighted; the fountain still presented the crystal mirror in which her charms may once have been reflected; the alabaster, it is true, had lost its whiteness; the basin beneath, overrun with weeds, had become the lurking-place of the lizard, but there was something in the very decay that enhanced the interest of the scene, speaking as it did of the mutability, the irrevocable lot of man and all his works."

In spite of warnings of the dangers of the place, Irving had his bed set up in the chamber beside this little garden. The first night was full of frightful terrors. The garden was dark and sinister. "There was a slight rustling noise overhead; a bat suddenly emerged from a broken panel of the ceiling, flitting about the room and athwart my solitary lamp; and as the fateful bird almost flouted my face with his noiseless wing, the grotesque faces carved in high relief in the cedar ceiling, whence he had emerged, seemed to mope and mow at me.

"Rousing myself, and half smiling at this temporary weakness, I resolved to brave it out in the true spirit of the hero of the enchanted house," says the narrator. So taking his lamp in his hand he started out to make a midnight tour of the palace.

"My own shadow, cast upon the wall, began to disturb me," he continues. "The echoes of my own footsteps along the corridors made me pause and look around. I was traversing scenes fraught with dismal recollections. One dark passage led down to the mosque where Yusef, the Moorish monarch, the finisher of the Alhambra, had been basely murdered. In another place I trod the gallery where another monarch had been struck down by the poniard of a relative whom he had thwarted in his love."

In a few nights, however, all this was changed; for the moon, which had been invisible, began to "roll in full splendor above the towers, pouring a flood of tempered light into every court and hall."

Says Irving, " I now felt the merit of the Arabic inscription on the walls—' How beauteous is this garden; where the flowers of the earth vie with the stars of heaven. What can compare with the vase of yon alabaster fountain filled with crystal water? Nothing but the moon in her fullness, shining in the midst of an unclouded sky!'"

"On such heavenly nights," he goes on, " I would sit for hours at my window inhaling the sweetness of the garden, and musing on the checkered fortunes of those whose history was dimly shadowed out in the elegant memorials around. Sometimes, when all was quiet, and the clock from the distant cathedral of Granada struck the midnight hour, I have sallied out on another tour and

wandered over the whole building; but how different from my first tour! No longer dark and mysterious; no longer peopled with shadowy foes; no
longer recalling scenes of violence and murder; all
was open, spacious, beautiful; everything called
up pleasing and romantic fancies; Lindaraxa once
more walked in her garden; the gay chivalry of
Moslem Granada once more glittered about the
Court of Lions!

" Who can do justice to a moonlight night in
such a climate and in such a place? The temper-
ature of a summer night in Andalusia is perfectly
ethereal. We seem lifted up into an ethereal
atmosphere ; we feel a serenity of soul, a
buoyancy of spirits, an elasticity of frame, which
render mere existence happiness. But when moonlight is added to all this, the effect is like enchantment. Under its plastic sway the Alhambra
seems to regain its pristine glories. Every rent
and chasm of time ; every moldering tint and
weather-stain is gone; the marble resumes its original whiteness; the long colonnades brighten in the
moonbeams; the halls are illuminated with a soft-

ened radiance—we tread the enchanted palace of an Arabian tale!"

When one may journey with such a companion, through a whole volume of enchantment and legend and moonlight, it is not strange that "The Alhambra" has been one of the most widely read books ever produced by an American writer.

CHAPTER XIV

THE LAST YEARS OF IRVING'S LIFE

Some people have thought that Irving's long residence abroad indicated that he did not care so much as he should for his native land. But the truth is, the years after his return to the United States were among the happiest of his life; and more and more he felt that here was his home.

In 1835 he purchased, as I have already said, a small piece of land on the Hudson, on which stood the Van Tassel house mentioned in the "Legend of Sleepy Hollow." It was an old Dutch cottage which had stood for so many years that it needed to be almost entirely rebuilt; and Irving spent a considerable sum of money to fit it up as his bachelor quarters. First he shared it with one of his bachelor brothers; but soon he invited his brother Ebenezer to come with his family of girls to occupy it with him.

As the years went on, Irving took a delight in this cottage that can hardly be expressed. At first he called it "Wolfert's Roost"; afterward the name was changed to "Sunnyside," the name by which it is still known. Little by little he bought more land, he planted trees, and cultivated flowers and vegetables. At one time he boasts that he has become so proficient in gardening that he can raise his own fruits and vegetables at a cost to him of little more than twice the market price.

During this period several books were published, among them a description of a tour on the prairies which he took soon after his return from abroad; a collection of "Legends of the Conquest of Spain" which had been lying in his trunk since his residence in the Alhambra seven or eight years before; and "Astoria," a book of Western life and adventure, describing John Jacob Astor's settlement on the Columbia river.

It was his wish to write a history of the conquest of Mexico, for which he had collected materials in Spain; but hearing that Prescott, the well-known American historian, was at work on the same subject, he gave it up to him.

The chief work of his later years was his "Life of George Washington." This was a great undertaking, of which he had often thought. He was actually at work on it for many years, and it was finally published only a short time before his death in 1859.

Irving's friends in the United States had long wished to give him some honor or distinction. He had been offered several public offices, among them the secretaryship of the navy; but he had declined them all. But in 1842, when Daniel Webster was secretary of state, Irving was nominated minister to Spain. It was Webster's idea, and he took great delight in carrying out his plan. After the notification of his nomination had been sent to Irving, and Webster thought time enough had elapsed for him to receive it, he remarked to a friend: "Washington Irving is now the most astonished man in the city of New York."

When Irving heard the news he seemed to think less of the distinction conferred upon him than of the unhappiness of being once more banished from his home. "It is hard—very hard," he murmured, half to himself; "yet," he added, whimsically enough (says his nephew), being struck with the seeming absurdity of such a view, "I must try to bear it. *God tempers the wind to the shorn lamb.*" Later, however, Irving speaks of this as the "crowning honor of his life."

He remained abroad four years, when he sent in his resignation, and hurried home to spend his last years at Sunnyside.

His first thought was to build an addition to his cottage, in order to have room for all his nieces and nephews. His enjoyment in every detail of the work was almost that of a boy. Though now an old man, he seemed as sunny and as gay as ever. Every one who knew him loved him; and all the people who now read his books must have the same affectionate fondness for this most delightful of companions.

In the United States he met both Dickens and Thackeray. His friendship with Dickens was begun by a letter which Irving wrote to the great novelist, enthusiastically praising his work. At once Dickens replied in a long letter, fairly bubbling over with delight and friendship. Here is a part of it:

"There is no man in the world who could have given me the heartfelt pleasure you have. There is no living writer, and there are very few among the dead, whose approbation I should feel so proud to earn. And with everything you have written upon my shelves, and in my thoughts, and in my heart of hearts, I may honestly and truly say so.

"I have been so accustomed to associate you with my pleasantest and happiest thoughts, and with my leisure hours, that I rush at once into full confidence with you, and fall, as it were, naturally, and by the very laws of gravity, into your open arms. . . . My dear Washington Irving, I cannot thank you enough for your cordial and generous praise, or tell you what deep and lasting gratification it has given me. I hope to have many letters from you, and to exchange a frequent correspondence. I send this to say so. . . .

"Always your faithful friend,

"CHARLES DICKENS."

The warmth of feeling which Dickens displays on receiving his first letter from Irving, we must all feel when we have become as well acquainted with Irving's works as Dickens was.

Washington Irving died on the 28th of November, 1859, at his dear Sunnyside, and now lies buried in a cemetery upon a hill near by, in a beautiful spot overlooking the Hudson river and Sleepy Hollow.

NOTE.—The thanks of the publishers are due to G. P. Putnam's Sons for kind permission to use extracts from the Works of Washington Irving.

THE STORY OF
EDGAR ALLAN POE

EDGAR ALLAN POE.

EDGAR ALLAN POE

CHAPTER I

THE ARTIST IN WORDS

Who has not felt the weird fascination of Poe's strangely beautiful poem "The Raven"? Perhaps on some stormy evening you have read it until the "silken, sad, uncertain rustling of each purple curtain" has "thrilled you, filled you, with fantastic terrors never felt before." That poem is the almost perfect mirror of the life of the man who wrote it—the most brilliant poetic genius in the whole range of American literature, the most unfortunate and unhappy.

Poe had a singular fate. When Longfellow and Bryant and Lowell and Holmes were winning their way to fame quietly and steadily, Poe was writing wonderful poems and wonderful stories, and more than that, he was inventing new principles and new artistic methods, on which other great writers in time to come should build their finest work ; yet he barely escaped starvation, and the critics made it appear that, compared with such men as Longfellow and Bryant, he was more notorious than really great.   Lowell in his "Fable for Critics," said:

"There comes Poe, ... three fifths of him genius, and two fifths sheer fudge,"

But now, fifty years after his death, we see how great a man Poe was.   Poe invented the modern art of short story writing.   His tales were translated into French by a famous writer named Charles Baudelaire.   Other French writers saw how fine they were and modeled their work upon them.   They learned the art of short story writing from Poe.   Then these French stories were translated into English, and English and American writers have imitated them and adopted similar methods of writing.

Conan Doyle's detective stories would probably never have been written had not Poe first composed "The Murders in the Rue Morgue"; and the stories of horror and fear so common to-day are possible because Poe wrote ''William Wilson,'' ''The Black Cat,'' and other stories of the same kind.

Have you ever learned to scan poetry? If you have, you know that the rules which tell you that a foot is composed of one long syllable and one short one, two short syllables and one long one, or whatever else it may be, are frequently disregarded. You know, too, that some lines are cut off short at the end, and others are made a little too long. Why is this permitted? In his '' Rationale of Verse,'' Poe explained all these things, and showed how the learned of past ages had made mistakes. In a subsequent chapter we shall see just what the relation between music and poetry is, and what Poe taught about the art of making poetry.

For years people thought that Poe's '' The Philosophy of Composition,'' in which he tells in what a cold-blooded way he wrote '' The Raven,'' was a joke; but in later times we have learned to understand what he meant and to know that he was very sensible in his methods of working.

When Poe was young he was not a very remarkable poet; but, as years went on and he learned more and more the art of writing, he rewrote and rewrote his verses until at last in conscious art he was almost, if not quite, the master poet of America.

CHAPTER II

POE'S FATHER AND MOTHER

Edgar Allan Poe was descended on his father's side from a Revolutionary hero, General David Poe. The Poes were a good family of Baltimore, where many of them still live as prominent citizens. It is said that General Poe was descended from one of Cromwell's officers, who received grants of land in Ireland. One of the poet's ancestors, John Poe, emigrated from Ireland to Pennsylvania; and from there the Poes went to Maryland. General Poe was an ardent patriot both before and during the Revolution.

General Poe's son David, the eldest, was not much like his father. In Baltimore he enjoyed himself with his friends and played at amateur theatricals with the Thespian Club. He was supposed to be studying law. For this purpose he went to live with an uncle in Augusta, Georgia; but his father soon heard that he had given up law to become an actor. General Poe was very angry and after that allowed the young man to shift for himself.

Edgar Allan Poe's mother was an English actress, whose mother had also been an actress. She was born at sea, and as she went with her mother on her travels from town to town, naturally the daughter learned the mother's art as a means of self-support, and in time became very successful.

At seventeen, her mother having married again, Elizabeth Arnold, for that was her name, was thrown upon her own resources. She joined a Philadelphia company, and remained with it for the next four years. In June, 1802, she acted in Baltimore, and perhaps it was there that David Poe, Jr., first saw her. She was pretty and gay, yet a good girl and a very fine actress.

She soon married a young Mr. Hopkins, who had been playing with the company, and for the following two years the young couple lived in Virginia. It was then that David Poe, Jr., having left his uncle's home at Augusta and gone on the stage in Charleston, joined the same company. He was not a very good actor; and he never rose to a high place in his profession.

In the following year Mr. Hopkins died, and a few months later young David Poe married Mrs. Hopkins, who had been Elizabeth Arnold.

Mr. and Mrs. David Poe were now husband and wife, and very poor, as most actors are. Soon after their marriage they went to Boston, and remained for some years. There Edgar Poe, their second son, was born, January 19, 1809.

While Edgar was still a little child his parents went to Richmond, Virginia, to fill an engagement in the theater there. Misfortune followed them. His father died in poverty, and his mother did not survive him long. Edgar and his brother and sister were thus left penniless orphans. But good friends took care of them.

Edgar was adopted by a Mrs. Allan, the wife of a wealthy man in the city of Richmond. She was very fond of the bright little boy, and as long as she lived he had a good home. He was petted and spoiled; but those were almost the only years of his life when he had plenty of money. He was very fond of his adoptive mother, and held her memory dear to the day of his death. He was now known as Edgar Allan.

CHAPTER III

YOUNG EDGAR ALLAN

Edgar was a beautiful child, with dark eyes, curly dark hair, and lively manners. At six he could read, draw, and dance. After dessert, sometimes they would put him up on the old-fashioned table, where he would make amusement for the company. He could speak pieces, too, and did it so well that people were astonished. He understood how to emphasize his words correctly. He had a pony and dogs, with which he ran about; and everywhere he was a great favorite.

In June, 1815, when Edgar was about six years old, his adoptive father and mother, with an aunt, went to England to stay several years. Before starting, Mr. Allan bought a Murray's reader, two Murray's spelling books, and another book to keep the little fellow busy on the long sailing voyage across the Atlantic; for at that time a trip to England occupied several weeks instead of a few days as now. When the family reached London and were settled down, Edgar was sent to a famous English school.

This school was at Stoke Newington, a quiet, old-fashioned country town, only a few miles out from London. Here was the house of Leicester, the favorite of Queen Elizabeth, whose story you may read in Scott's "Kenilworth"; and here too was the house of Anne Boleyn's ill-fated lover, Earl Percy.

The Manor House School, as it was called, was in a quaint and very old building, with high walls about the grounds, and great spiked, iron-studded gates. Here the boys lived and studied, seldom returning home, and seldom going outside the grounds, except when they went with a teacher.

In this strange school, Edgar Allan lived and studied for five years. The schoolroom was long, narrow, and low; it was ceiled with dark oak, and had Gothic windows. The desks were black and irregular, covered with the names and initials which the boys had cut with their jackknives. In the corners were what might be called boxes, where sat the masters—one of them Eugene Aram, the criminal made famous in one of Bulwer's romances. Back of the schoolroom, reached by winding, narrow passages, were the bedrooms, one of which Poe occupied. When the boys went out to walk they passed under the giant elms, amid which once lived Shakespeare's friend Essex, and they gazed up at the thick walls, deep windows, and doors massive with locks and bars, behind which the author of Robinson Crusoe wrote some of his famous works.

Within the walls of this school a large number of boys had a little world all to themselves; they had their societies and their games and their tricks, along with hard work in Latin and French and mathematics; and though such work may seem monotonous and dreary, they managed to enjoy it. Poe has described his life here very carefully in his famous story of "William Wilson." "Oh, a fine time were those years of iron!" says he. The life produced a deep impression on his mind, and molded it for the strange, weird poetry and fiction which in later years he was to write.

At last, in 1820, the Allans returned with Edgar to their home in Richmond, Virginia. The lad now added his own name to that of Edgar Allan, and became known as Edgar Allan Poe.

He was at once sent to the English and Classical School of Joseph H. Clarke, where he prepared for college. He did not study very hard, but was bright and quick, and at one time stood at the head of his class with but one rival. He was a great athlete, too, being a good runner and jumper and boxer. He was a remarkable swimmer, and it is stated that he once swam six miles in the James River, against a strong tide in a hot sun, and then walked back without seeming in the least tired.

He was slight in figure, but robust and tough, and was a very decided character among his classmates. He took part in the debating society, where he was prominent, and was known as a versifier of both love poems and satire. When Master Clarke retired, in 1823, Poe read an English ode addressed to the outgoing principal.

One of his friends said of him at this time that he was "self-willed, capricious, inclined to be imperious, and though of generous impulses, not steadily kind, nor even amiable." Part of this temper on his part may have come from the fact that the aristocratic boys of the school hinted that his father and mother had not been of the best people. They knew, however, that Mr. Allan belonged to the best society; and it was chiefly Edgar's imperious manners that made some of them shun him. He had friends, however, and Mr. Allan gave him money liberally.

It was at this time that he found and lost his first sympathetic friend.

This was Mrs. Jane Stith Stanard, the mother of one of his younger schoolmates. When one day he went home with this friend, he met Mrs. Stanard, a lovely, gentle, and gracious woman, was thrilled by the tenderness of her tones and her sympathetic manner toward him, and immediately made her his boyhood friend and confidante. To his great grief, however, she died not very long afterward. When she was gone he visited her grave time after time, and in after years when he was unhappy he often thought and spoke of her.

CHAPTER IV

COLLEGE LIFE

Poe left the English and Classical School in March, 1825, and spent the next few months in studying with a private tutor.

On the 14th of February, 1826, he wrote his name and the place and date of his birth, in the matriculation book of the University of Virginia, the famous college founded by Jefferson and opened about a year before.

Poe is described at this time as short, thickset, bowlegged, with the rapid and jerky gait of an English boy. His face, surrounded by dark curly hair, wore a grave, half-melancholy look ; but it would light up expressively when he talked. He was a noted walker; and being the adopted child of a rich man, he dressed well and carried himself proudly. He studied Latin, Greek, French, Spanish, and Italian, and stood well in his classes. At the end of the year he went home with the highest honors in Latin and French.

Before the term closed, however, Mr. Allan went up to investigate some stories of Poe's wildness that had reached him, and found that besides other debts, Poe owed two thousand dollars in "debts of honor"—that is, gambling debts. Mr. Allan paid all but the latter, and quietly determined that as soon as the term closed, Poe's college life should end.

Poe was, however, a studious and well-behaved young man in the opinion of the professors, and

he was never found guilty of any serious mis-
conduct. He was fond of wandering over the
Ragged Mountains, whither he went alone or
with only a dog, and he delighted to fancy that he
was the very first white person to penetrate some
lonely glen or ravine.

He was also something of an artist, and deco-
rated his rooms with charcoal sketches. He and
a classmate bought a volume of Byron with steel
engravings in it. The next time his friend went
to see Poe he found him copying one of these on
the ceiling, and he continued this until he had covered the whole of the walls with figures that were
said to be artistic and striking.

CHAPTER V

FORTUNE CHANGES

At the age of eighteen there came a change
in Poe's life. Until then he had been a petted
child in a wealthy family. Mr. Allan did not have
that affection for him which Mrs. Allan had. He

did not understand the boy's peculiar and erratic nature, and was particularly displeased when he found that Edgar had run into debt at college. There was an angry scene between the two, and Edgar was told that he must leave the university and go into the counting-room. It appears that he made some attempt to tie himself down to figures and accounts and business routine; but as he had not been brought up to this kind of life, he soon tired of it, and decided to go into the world to seek his own fortune. He went to Boston, where he published a volume of poetry.

In the preface to this volume, Poe says that the poems were written before he was fourteen. Though this may not be strictly true, there is little doubt that some of them were. While he was still at school he had collected enough of his poems to make a volume, and Mr. Allan had taken them up to the master of the English and Classical School to get his advice about publishing them. This gentleman advised against it on the ground that it would make Edgar conceited,—a fault from which he was already suffering. As soon as he was free to do as he pleased, therefore, it was natural that he should rewrite his poems and publish them.

The volume was entitled ''Tamerlane and Other Poems. By a Bostonian.'' It was published by a young printer named Calvin Thomas, and was a thin little book, not very attractive in appearance. Several of the pieces then published are now included in Poe's collected works, but they have been greatly changed.

Naturally the poems of an obscure young man did not sell, and the volume was soon suppressed— Poe says ''for private reasons.'' The ''private reasons'' were doubtless merely the fact that the book was a complete failure, and the young, proud poet was much ashamed that he could not sell even a dozen copies—possibly not even one.

The little money Poe had was now spent, and he was obliged to do something to keep from starvation. The only chance he saw was to enlist in the army. He did so under the name of Edgar A. Perry, and the record of his service may be found in the War Department of our government at Washington. He was assigned to Battery H, First Artillery, and conducted himself so well that he was promoted from the ranks to be sergeant-major. From Boston the company was sent to Charleston, South Carolina, and a year later to Fortress Monroe, Virginia.

From Fortress Monroe Poe wrote to Mr. Allan for the first time. He soon afterwards learned of the illness of Mrs. Allan, who died February 28, 1829. He got leave of absence to attend her funeral, and went to Richmond.

Poe was such a bright young man that it seemed a pity for him to remain in the ranks, when he might become an officer; therefore it was suggested that he be sent to West Point. Mr. Allan agreed to help him; but it is said that, after the death of Mrs. Allan, he no longer entertained any affection for Edgar. In a letter to the Secretary of War, he said: "Frankly, sir, I do declare that he is no relation to me whatever; that I have many in whom I have taken an active interest to promote theirs; with no other feeling than that, every man is my care, if he be in distress. For myself I ask nothing, but I do request your kindness to aid this youth in the promotion of his future prospects."

Poe did not like the life at West Point in the least, though he amused his mates by writing satirical verses about the professors. After a few months he asked to be discharged; but Mr. Allan would not consent. So Poe made up his mind that he would have himself expelled. He stayed away from parade, roll-call, and guard duty. As a court-martial was then in session, he was summoned before it. He denied the most flagrant charge against him; but this only made his case worse, and he was expelled from the academy.

CHAPTER VI

LIVING BY LITERATURE

Once more the young poet found himself cast out on the world, without home or friends. He could hope for nothing more from Mr. Allan, after his disgrace at the military academy, and

he had found out that army life was not so fine
a refuge from starvation as he had thought it.
He was a proud, melancholy young man, and in
school and college had learned many bad habits.
He had no trade nor practical knowledge of any
kind of work, though he was quick and ingenious.
He had studied the art of writing, and this
alone offered him the means of earning a livelihood. How poor and precarious a chance it was,
we shall see as we go on.

While waiting for appointment to the Military
Academy the preceding year, Poe had made acquaintance with his father's relatives in Baltimore.
He formed some literary connections there, and had
a volume of his poems published. It was entitled
''Al Aaraaf, Tamerlane, and Minor Poems, by
Edgar A. Poe.'' ''Al Aaraaf'' was a poem about
a star that a great astronomer had seen blaze
forth and then disappear.

When he left West Point in April, 1831,
nearly two years after the publication of his Baltimore volume, Poe was short of money; and to
supply his needs his fellow-students subscribed for

a new edition of his poems. For this, seventy-five cents was stopped out of the pay of each, and a publisher in New York agreed to issue the book in good style. The cadets thought his volume would contain the many funny squibs he had written on the professors; but they were disappointed.

Poe next went to Baltimore. There he tried to get employment in vain. Friends helped him, but it was some time before he made his first literary success.

It happened at last that a weekly paper called the *Saturday Visiter* was started in Baltimore. To give the paper popularity, two prizes were offered, one of a hundred dollars for the best short story, and the other of fifty for the best poem. Poe tried for both. He had six short stories, which he copied in a neat little manuscript volume entitled "Tales of the Folio Club." The poem he sent was "The Coliseum."

The judges were well-known gentlemen of the city of Baltimore, one of whom, John P. Kennedy, afterward became Poe's intimate friend. When they met they looked over several stories, which did not interest them very much. They then came to the "Tales of the Folio Club." One was read aloud, and the three gentlemen were so much interested that they kept on till they had read all, and at once decided to give the prize to one of these. They chose Poe's famous story "A MS. Found in a Bottle." Afterward they decided that his poem was the best submitted; but noticing that it was in the same handwriting as the stories, they thought it best to give the prize to another. When they made their report they greatly complimented the stories Poe had sent in, and said they should be published in a volume.

We have said that one of the judges, Mr. Kennedy, became Poe's friend. To show how very poor Poe was, I copy this passage from Mr. Kennedy's diary: "It was many years ago that I found Poe in Baltimore in a state of starvation. I gave him clothing, free access to my table, and the use of a horse for exercise whenever he chose; in fact, I brought him up from the very verge of despair."

Here, too, is an extract from a letter from Poe to Mr. Kennedy:

"Your invitation to dinner has wounded me to the quick. I cannot come for reasons of the most humiliating nature—my personal appearance. You may imagine my mortification in making this disclosure to you, but it is necessary."

Mr. Kennedy did all that a friend could do for the future poet and story-writer. Says Poe: "He has been at all times a true friend to me—he was the first true friend I ever had—I am indebted to him for *life itself*."

Poe now contributed regularly to the *Saturday Visiter*, its young editor, Lambert A. Wilmer, becoming his friend and constant companion. It is said that at this time he dressed very neatly, though inexpensively, "wore Byron collars and a black stock, and looked the poet all over."

CHAPTER VII

POE'S EARLY POETRY

We have seen how persistently Poe clung to his poetry. Three times he published the little volume of his verses, revising, enlarging, and strengthening. In those days there was no market for poetic writing, and as Poe wrote in a strange, weird style, it is not remarkable that no one took any notice of the contents of his little volumes. It was his own opinion, however, that these early poems contained more real poetic imagination than his later successes, and it is perhaps as well that we should begin our study of Poe with some of the first fruits of his genius.

First let us read that most pathetic of autobiographical poems, ''Alone.'' With strange sincerity and directness the poet tells us how his spirit grew and learned the burden of its melancholy, yet scintillating song:

From childhood's hour I have not been
As others were,—I have not seen
As others saw,—I could not bring
My passions from a common spring.
From the same source I have not taken
My sorrow; I could not awaken
My heart to joy at the same tone;
And all I loved, *I* loved alone.
Then—in my childhood—in the dawn
Of a most stormy life was drawn

From every depth of good and ill
The mystery which binds me still:
From the torrent, or the fountain,
From the red cliff of the mountain,
From the sun that round me rolled
In its autumn tint of gold,—
From the lightning in the sky
As it passed me flying by,—
From the thunder and the storm,
And the cloud that took the form
(When the rest of heaven was blue)
Of a demon in my view.

As a poem written in early youth we should not expect this to be as perfect as "The Raven," for instance. Let us see if we can find some of its faults, as well as some of its beauties:

First, we notice that it ends rather abruptly, as if it were unfinished. In his essay on "The Poetic Principle" Poe pointed out that many a poem fails of its effect by being too short. It must not be so long that one is wearied out before it can be read through; at the same time it must be long enough to convey the whole of the idea. This poem of his own is an example of the fault he himself pointed out. It is too short to give us clear ideas of all he evidently had in his mind.

We notice, also, that it is rhymed in couplets, that is, every two lines are rhymed together. Now the couplets in the last half of the poem seem to strike the ear with more satisfaction than those in the first part. For instance, we are pleased with the sound of these lines:

> From the torrent, or the fountain,
> From the red cliff of the mountain.

But in some of the lines the pauses of punctuation do not come at the right points to make smooth reading:

> From the same source I have not taken
> My sorrow; I could not awaken
> My heart to joy at the same tone;
> And all I loved, *I* loved alone.

The semicolon after "sorrow" should have come at the end of the line instead of in the middle. Poe had not yet learned the secret of the rhythmic flow which we find in such perfection in "The Bells," for instance.

But in the last part of the poem we find a beauty of image and comparison that thrills us, and something of thàt strange, weird suggestiveness which was characteristic of all of Poe's poetry, the thing he has in common with no other poet.

This weird suggestiveness is found in still greater vividness in another poem entitled "The Lake." In this, besides, we see how Poe had a sort of fascination for the horrible. Notice how he says:

> Yet that terror was not fright,
> But a tremulous delight.

Here is the complete poem. The young student of poetry may study it for himself, and discover, if he can, its shortcomings, as we have pointed out the faults in the poem "Alone."

> In spring of youth it was my lot
> To haunt of the wide world a spot
> The which I could not love the less,— ·
> So lovely was the loveliness
> Of a wild lake, with black rock bound,
> And the tall pines that towered around.
> But when the night had thrown her pall
> Upon that spot as upon all,

And the mystic wind went by
Murmuring in melody,—
Then,—ah, then I would awake
To the terror of the lone lake.
Yet that terror was not fright,
But a tremulous delight,—
A feeling not the jeweled mine
Could teach or bribe me to define,—
Nor Love—although the Love were thine.

Death was in that poisonous wave,
And its gulf a fitting grave
For him who thence could solace bring
To his lone imagining,—
Whose solitary soul could make
An Eden of that dim lake.

These poems are chiefly interesting as they give us some idea of the nature of the young poet's mind. Poe had what may be called a scientific mind, infused through and through with poetry. At times he was exact, keen-minded, and patient as the scientist; then again he wandered away into mere fanciful suggestion of things that "never were on land or sea." His scientific turn we see in his detective stories; his poetic nature we see struggling against this intellectual exactness in the following sonnet:

Science!   True daughter of Old Time thou art!
  Who alterest all things with thy peering eyes.
Why preyest thou upon the poet's heart,
  Vulture, whose wings are dull realities?
How should he love thee? or how deem thee wise,
  Who wouldst not leave him in his wandering
To seek for treasure in the jeweled skies,
  Albeit he soared with an undaunted wing?
Hast thou not dragged Diana from her car?
  And driven the Hamadryad from the wood
To seek a shelter in some happier star?
  Hast thou not torn the Naiad from her flood,
The Elfin·from the green grass, and from me
The summer dream beneath the tamarind tree?

CHAPTER VIII

POE'S CHILD WIFE

While Poe was in Baltimore, after he had begun to earn something by his pen, he went to live with his aunt, Mrs. Clemm.   She was very poor, and whatever Poe earned went toward the support of the whole family, which included not only Poe and his aunt, but her young daughter Virginia, at this time only eleven years of age.

Virginia was an exceedingly delicate and beautiful girl. She had dark hair and eyes, and a fine, transparent complexion. She was very modest and quiet; but she had a fine mind, and a very sweet and winning manner. She had also a poetic nature, and became an accomplished musician.

Mrs. Clemm, on the other hand, was a large, coarsely formed woman, and it seemed impossible that she could be the mother of so delicate and graceful a girl. She was very faithful and hard-working, however, and sincerely devoted to Poe as well as to her daughter. She had the business ability to manage Poe's small income in the best way, and made for him a home that would have been extremely happy had it not been for poverty and other misfortunes.

While Poe lived in Baltimore he would go out to walk nearly every day with the editor of the *Saturday Visiter;* but he sometimes walked alone or with Virginia.

After a time the young poet and story-writer decided to go to Richmond, his early home. He had many friends there, who welcomed him back, and a good position was offered him. The *Southern Literary Messenger* had been started by a Mr. White, and Poe was made assistant editor.

He had become very much attached to Mrs. Clemm and Virginia while in Baltimore, and now wished to marry Virginia. She was but fourteen years of age,—indeed, not quite fourteen,—and Mrs. Clemm's friends thought the girl too young to marry. But Poe gained the mother's consent, and he and Virginia were united in May, 1836.

Virginia was Poe's ideal of womanhood, and we find her figuring as the model for nearly all the heroines of his poems. In a letter after the death of both Virginia and her poet husband, Mrs. Clemm wrote, "She was an excellent linguist and a perfect musician, and she was very beautiful. How often has Eddie said, 'I see no one so beautiful as my sweet little wife.'" Poe undertook her education as soon as they were married, and was very proud of her brilliant accomplishments.

As she was the source of his greatest happiness, her loss was the occasion of his greatest sorrow. A year after their marriage she burst a blood vessel while singing. The following extract from a letter of Poe's to a friend will explain how this misfortune affected him.

"You say," he writes, "'Can you hint to me what was the terrible evil which caused the irregularities so profoundly lamented?' Yes, I can do more than hint. This 'evil' was the greatest which can befall a man. Six years ago, a wife, whom I loved as no man ever loved before, ruptured a blood vessel in singing. Her life was despaired of. I took leave of her forever, and underwent all the agonies of her death. She recovered partially and I again hoped. At the end of a year the blood vessel broke again. I went through precisely the same scene.—Then again—again—and even once again, at varying intervals. Each time I felt all the agonies of her death—and at each accession of her disorder I loved her more dearly and clung to her life with more desperate pertinacity."

Virginia gradually grew worse and finally died at
their home at Fordham, near New York.   After
this sad event Poe wrote a poem which is a sort
of requiem for her death.   It was not published
during his life, but after his death it appeared
in the *New York Tribune*.   Immediately it took
rank as one of the three greatest poems Poe ever
wrote.   It is long enough to be complete, it has
none of those metrical imperfections found in his
earlier poems, and it possesses in a wonderful
degree that haunting thrill so characteristic of all
the best things Poe wrote.   Moreover, it has
a musical flow surpassing any other of Poe's poems
except ''The Bells,'' and in some respects it is
even more pleasing to the ear when read aloud
than is ''The Bells.''

ANNABEL LEE.

It was many and many a year ago,
  In a kingdom by the sea,
That a maiden there lived whom you may know
  By the name of Annabel Lee;
And this maiden she lived with no other thought
  Than to love and be loved by me.

I was a child and *she* was a child,
   In this kingdom by the sea:
But we loved with a love that was more than love,—
   I and my Annabel Lee;
With a love that the winged seraphs of heaven
   Coveted her and me.

And this was the reason that, long ago,
   In this kingdom by the sea,
A wind blew out of a cloud, chilling
   My beautiful Annabel Lee;
So that her highborn kinsmen came
   And bore her away from me,
To shut her up in a sepulcher
   In this kingdom by the sea.

The angels, not half so happy in heaven,
   Went envying her and me,—
Yes!—that was the reason (as all men know,
   In this kingdom by the sea)
That the wind came out of the cloud by night,
   Chilling and killing my Annabel Lee.

But our love it was stronger by far than the love
   Of those who were older than we,—
   Of many far wiser than we;
And neither the angels in heaven above,

Nor the demons down under the sea,
Can ever dissever my soul from the soul
  Of the beautiful Annabel Lee:

For the moon never beams without bringing me dreams
  Of the beautiful Annabel Lee;
And the stars never rise but I feel the bright eyes
  Of the beautiful Annabel Lee;
And so, all the night-tide, I lie down by the side
Of my darling—my darling—my life and my bride,
  In the sepulcher there by the sea,
  In her tomb by the sounding sea.

CHAPTER IX

POE'S LITERARY HISTORY

As assistant editor of the *Southern Literary Messenger*, Poe achieved great literary success. In this paper he began those spirited criticisms of the writers of the day, which attracted attention everywhere. He also published numerous stories. Poetry was almost completely abandoned for prose.

The circulation of the magazine increased by the thousands, and there could be no doubt that its

success was due chiefly to Poe.   At first his salary
was ten dollars a week ; later, it was raised to fifteen dollars, and was to have been raised to
twenty, but Poe suddenly resigned his position.
Precisely why he did this is not known.

Experiences similar to that with the *Southern
Literary Messenger* were repeated many times
afterward, during his literary career. Just as he was
getting well settled at his work, he would have
some difficulty with the proprietor, or commit some
indiscretion, and then he must find some other place.
In those days, when a great New York daily paper
like Bryant's *Evening Post* could be bought for from
$5,000 to $10,000, there was not much money
to be made in publishing or in literature.   To
make money, Poe should have been a business
man, and he was not so in any sense.   Many another literary man, even in our own times, has had
similar misfortunes, even without those faults of
character and that fatality for falling out with everything and everybody which distinguished Poe.

From Richmond, Poe went with his family to
New York, where Mrs. Clemm supported the house-

hold by keeping boarders. Poe himself spent the winter chiefly in writing "The Narrative of Arthur Gordon Pym," a tale of the sea, which was first published by Messrs. Harper and Brothers.

From New York he went to Philadelphia, where he wrote various magazine articles and stories, and did part of the work of preparing a school text-book on "Conchology." He soon became associate editor of *The Gentleman's Magazine* with its proprietor Burton. The following year, 1840, his first volume of stories was published, under the title, "Tales of the Grotesque and Arabesque." The volume was not a popular success. An edition of seven hundred and fifty copies was barely disposed of, and all that Poe received was twenty copies for distribution among his friends.

His connection with Burton's magazine did not last above a year. Burton had been a comic actor, and offered prizes which Poe says he never intended to pay. Poe's remarks on this transaction caused the rupture.

Poe had already been thinking about starting a periodical of his own, and now he sent out the prospectus of *The Penn Magazine*. To found a magazine which should be better and higher in literary art than any other in America was his lifelong ambition. He tried again and again to do this, first with *The Penn Magazine*, and later with a periodical to be called *The Stylus*. He never succeeded, however.

George R. Graham, proprietor of the *Saturday Evening Post*, now bought *The Gentleman's Magazine*, united it with a periodical of his own called *The Casket*, and named the new venture *Graham's Magazine*. Of this Poe soon became the editor.

After Poe's death, Mr. Graham published an article in which he said that, while he was in Philadelphia, Poe seemed to think only of the happiness and welfare of his family. There were but two things for which he cared to have money—to give them comforts and to start a magazine of his own. He never spent any money on himself. Everything was intrusted to Mrs. Clemm, who managed all his household affairs. His love for his wife was a sort of rapturous worship of the spirit of beauty, which he felt was fading before his eyes. "I have seen him," says Mr. Graham, "hovering around her when she was ill, with all the fond fear and tender anxiety of a mother for her first-born—her slightest cough causing him a shudder, a heart chill, that was visible. I rode out one summer evening with them, and the remembrance of his watchful eyes, eagerly bent upon the slightest change of hue in that loved face, haunts me yet as the memory of a sad strain. It was this hourly anticipation of her loss which made him a sad and thoughtful man, and lent a mournful melody to his undying song."

At last he left Philadelphia and returned to New York, where he remained for the rest' of his life. This is the childlike way he writes to his mother-in-law concerning the journey:

"My Dear Muddy,

"We have just this minute done breakfast, and I now sit down to write you about everything. * * * In the first place, we arrived safe at Walnut St. wharf. The driver wanted to make me pay a dollar, but I wouldn't. Then I had to pay a boy a levy to put the trunks in the baggage car.

In the meantime I took Sis [Virginia] in the Depot
Hotel. * * * We went in the cars to Amboy,
* * * and then took the steamboat the rest of
the way. Sissy coughed none at all. I left her on
board the boat. * * * Then I went up Green-
wich St. and soon found a boarding house. * * *
I made a bargain in a few minutes and then got
a hack and went for Sis. * * * When we got
to the house we had to wait about half an hour
before the room was ready. The house is old and
looks buggy, * * * the cheapest board I ever
knew, taking into consideration the central situation and the *living*. I wish Kate [Catterina, the
cat] could see it—she would faint."

They had a little cottage at Fordham, in the
country just out of New York. It was a very humble place, but the scenery about it was beautiful.
Poe himself became ill, and his dear Virginia was
dying of consumption. They were so poor that
friends had to help them. One of these friends
wrote :

" There was no clothing on the bed, which was
only straw, but a snow-white counterpane and

sheets. The weather was cold and the sick lady had the dreadful chills that accompany the hectic fever of consumption. She lay on the bed wrapped in her husband's great-coat, with a large tortoise-shell cat in her bosom."

On one Saturday in January, 1847, Virginia died. Her husband, wrapped in the military cloak that had once covered her, followed the body to the tomb in the family vault of the Valentines, relatives of the family.

CHAPTER X

POE AS A STORY-WRITER

Next to "The Raven," Poe's most famous work is that fascinating story, "The Gold-Bug," perhaps the best detective story that was ever written, for it is based on logical principles which are instructive as well as interesting. Poe's powerful mind was always analyzing and inventing. It is these inventions and discoveries of his which make him famous.

The story of the gold-bug is that of a man who finds a piece of parchment on which is a secret writing telling where Captain Kidd hid his treasure off the coast of South Carolina. The gold-beetle has nothing whatever to do with the real story, and is only introduced to mystify. It is one of the principles of all conjuring tricks to have something to divert the attention. Poe's detective story is a sort of conjuring trick, but it is all the more interesting because he fully explains it.

Cryptographs are systems of secret writing. The letter *e* is represented by some strange character, perhaps the figure 8. In "The Gold-Bug" *t* is a semicolon and *h* is 4, so that ;48 means *the*. Sometimes the letter *e* is represented by several signs, any one of which the writer may use; and perhaps the word *the*, which occurs so often, is represented by a single character, like *x*. Often, too, the words are run together, so that at first sight you cannot tell where one word begins and another ends.

Solving a cryptograph is like doing a mathematical problem, and Poe was very clever at it.

He published a series of articles on "Cryptography" or systems of secret writing, in *Alexander's Weekly Messenger*, and challenged any reader to send in a cipher which he could not translate into ordinary language. Hundreds were sent to him, and he solved them all, though it took up a great deal of his time.

In the same line with this was another feat of his. Dickens's story, "Barnaby Rudge," was coming out in parts from week to week, as a serial publication. From the first chapters Poe calculated what the outcome of the plot would be, and published it in the *Saturday Evening Post.* He guessed the story so accurately that Dickens was greatly surprised and asked him if he were the devil.

Again at a later date Poe wrote a remarkable story, "The Mystery of Marie Roget." A young girl had been murdered in New York. The newspapers were full of accounts of the crime, but the police could get no clew to the murderers. In Poe's story he wrote out exactly what happened on the night of the murder, and explained the whole

thing, as if he were an expert detective. Afterward, by the confessions of two of the participants,
it was proved that his solution of the mystery was
almost exactly the truth.

"The Gold-Bug" was not published until some-
time later, but it was as editor of *Graham's Magazine* that Poe first became known as a writer of
detective stories. One of the most famous is "The
Murders of the Rue Morgue." It is an imaginary
story, but none the less interesting. A murder was
committed in Paris by an orang-outang, which
had climbed in at a window and then closed the
window behind it. The police could find no clew;
but the hero of Poe's story follows the facts out by
a number of clever observations of small facts.

"The Gold-Bug" seems to have been written in
1842 for Poe's projected magazine, *The Stylus*.
F. O. C. Darley, the well-known artist, was to draw
pictures for it at seven dollars each. Poe himself
took to him the manuscript of "The Gold-Bug"
and that of "The Black Cat."

As this magazine was never published, the story
of "The Gold-Bug" was sent to Graham some

time after Poe had left him ; but he did not like it, and made some criticisms upon it. Poe got it back from Graham in order to submit it for a prize of $100 offered by *The Dollar Newspaper*. It won the prize, and became Poe's most popular story.

CHAPTER XI

HOW "THE RAVEN" WAS WRITTEN

"The Raven" was published in New York just two years before Mrs. Poe died; it instantly made its author famous, although it brought him little or no money. It is said that he was paid only ten dollars for the poem; but as soon as it appeared it was the talk of the nation,—being copied into almost every newspaper. Poe had written and published many other poems, but none of them had attracted much attention.

We have spoken of Poe as a story-writer, and now in "The Raven" we see him a great poet.

It is not unusual to think of poetry as the work of inspiration or genius; but how it is written, nobody knows. Poe maintained that literary art is some-thing that can be studied and learned. To illustrate this he told how he wrote "The Raven." Some people considered this a sort of joke; but it was not. When Poe began to write, his work was not at all good; as years went on, he learned by patient practice to write well. It was more than anything else this long course of training that made him so great.

The essay in which he tells how he wrote "The Raven," begins by saying that when he thought of writing it he decided that it must not be too long nor too short. It must be short enough so that one could read it through at a sitting; but also it must be long enough to express fully the idea which he had in mind.

Then, it must be beautiful. All true poetry is about beauty. It doesn't teach anything useful, or analyze anything, but it simply makes the reader feel a certain effect. When you read "The Raven" you hardly know what the poet is saying; but you feel the ghostly scene, and it makes you shudder; and there is a strange fascination about it that makes you like it, even if it is horrible.

He goes on to say that he decided to have a refrain at the end of each stanza, the single word "Nevermore." At first he thought he would have a parrot utter it; but a raven can talk as well as a parrot, and is more picturesque. The most striking subject he could think of was the death of a beautiful woman—this he felt to be so because of his own impressions concerning the approaching death of his sweet wife.

Besides this, Poe said that poetry and music are much alike, and he tried to have his poem produce the effect of solemn music. All his best poetry is very much like music.

With these materials at his command, he now turned his attention to the construction of the poem. He would ask questions, and the raven would always reply by croaking "Nevermore." As an answer to some questions, this would sound very terrible. Says he: "I first established in my mind the climax, or concluding query,—that query in reply to which the word 'nevermore' should involve the utmost conceivable amount of sorrow and despair. Here, then, the poem may be said to have its beginning—at the end, where all works of art should begin—for it was here, at this point of my preconsiderations, that I first put pen to paper in the composition of the stanza:—

" ' Prophet!' said I, ' thing of evil!—prophet still, if bird
          or devil!
By the heaven that bends above us—by that God we both
          adore!—
Tell this soul with sorrow laden, if, within the distant
          Aidenn,
It shall clasp a sainted maiden whom the angels name
          Lenore,—
Clasp a rare and radiant maiden whom the angels name
          Lenore.'
                    Quoth the Raven, ' Nevermore.' "

This principle of beginning at the end or climax to write a poem or story was one so important that Poe insisted on it at great length. In the " Murders in the Rue Morgue " the author necessarily began at the end, imagined the solution of the mystery, and gradually worked back to the beginning, bringing in his detective after every-thing had been carefully constructed for him, though to the ordinary reader of the story it seems as if the detective came to a real mystery.

It may be observed that all of Poe's stories and poems are built up about some principle of the mind. They illustrate how the mind works. After the principle is stated the illustration is given.

Can anything be more important and interesting than to know how the mind thinks, how it is inspired with terror or love or a sense of beauty? If you know just how the mind of a man works in regard to these things, you can yourself create the conditions which will make others laugh or cry, be filled with horror, or overflow with a sense of divine holiness. Ordinary story-tellers and ordinary poets write poems or stories that are pretty and amusing; but it is only a master like Poe who writes to illustrate and explain some great principle. His stories teach us how we may go about producing similar effects in the affairs of life. We wish success in business, in society, in politics. To gain it we must make people think and feel as we think and feel. To do that we must understand the principles on which men's minds work, and no poet or writer analyzed and illustrated those principles so clearly as Poe.

CHAPTER XII

MUSIC AND POETRY

Poe always maintained that music and poetry are very near of kin, and in nearly all his greatest poems he seems to write in such a way as to produce the impression of music. As you read his verses you seem to hear a musical accompaniment to the words, which runs through the very sounds of the words themselves.

Poe explained that poetry and music are alike in that both obey absolute laws of time, and that the laws of time or rhythm in poetry are just as exact as the laws of time in music. He wrote an essay entitled "The Rationale of Verse," in which he demonstrated that all the rules for scanning poetry are defective. Every one knows that the ordinary rules for meter have numerous exceptions, but that if the rules were exact in the first place, there would be no exceptions.

Perhaps you know something about musical notes. If so, a simple illustration will show you what "feet" in poetry are. You have perhaps been taught that a "foot" in verse is an accented syllable with one or more unaccented syllables, and you scan poetry by marking all the accented syllables. In Latin, poetry was scanned by marking long vowels and short. Let us scan the first two lines of "The Raven":

"Ónce up | ón a | mídnight | dréary, ‖ whíle I | póndered | wéak and | wéary,
Óver | mány a | quáint and | cúrious | vólume | óf for | gótten | lóre."

Observe that most of the feet have two syllables each, while two have three. But if you read the lines in a natural tone you will see that you give just as much time to one foot as to another, and where there are three syllables they are short and can be

pronounced quickly. Some syllables take more
time to pronounce than other syllables; and to
accent a syllable simply means to give it more
time in pronouncing. In music, time is accurately represented by notes, and a bar of music
always contains exactly the same amount of time,
no matter how it is divided by the notes; for if
you wish, in place of a half note you can use two
quarter notes, or in place of a quarter note you
can use two eighth notes. Represented in music,
our lines will be as follows:

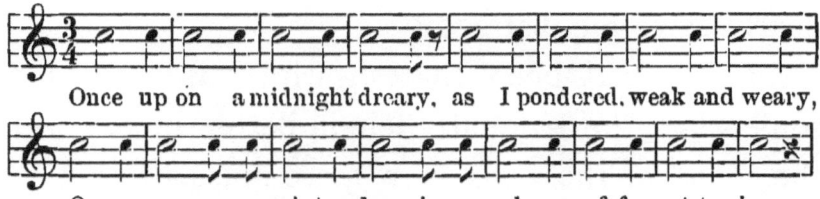

Once up on a midnight dreary, as I pondered, weak and weary,

O - ver man-y a quaint and cur-i - ous vol-ume of for-got-ten lore.

We see this still further illustrated in a poem of
Tennyson's, where a foot consists of but one long
syllable, thus:

Break, break, break, On thy cold grey stones, O sea!

One of Poe's greatest poems, "The Bells," was
written for the express purpose of imitating music

in verse. The story of how it was first written is as follows:

Poe went one Sunday morning to call on a lady friend of his, Mrs. Shaw, who was something of a physician and had been very kind to his wife. It was a bright morning, and the church bells were ringing. For all that, Poe felt moody, and the church bells seemed to jangle.

"I must write a poem," said he, "and I haven't an idea in my head. For some reason the bells seem frightfully out of tune this morning, and nearly drive me distracted."

After he had been chatting with Mrs. Shaw for some time, he evidently felt in better mood, and the sound of the bells grew more musical; or perhaps their actual sound had stopped and his imagination suggested bells that were indeed musical.

As he kept on complaining about his inability to write a poem, Mrs. Shaw placed pen and ink and paper before him, first writing at the top of a sheet the title, "The Bells, by E. A. Poe." Underneath she wrote, "The bells, the little silver bells." Poe caught the idea, and immediately wrote the first draft of the following stanza. According to his habit he rewrote this poem many, many times. The original stanza began with the words Mrs. Shaw had written. Here are the verses as they may now be read in Poe's works:

> Hear the sledges with the bells—
> Silver bells!
> What a world of merriment their melody foretells!
> How they tinkle, tinkle, tinkle,
> In the icy air of night!
> While the stars that oversprinkle
> All the heaven, seem to twinkle
> With a crystalline delight;
> Keeping time, time, time,
> In a sort of Runic rhyme
> To the tintinnabulation that so musically wells
> From the bells, bells, bells, bells,
> Bells, bells, bells,—
> From the jingling and the tinkling of the bells.

Mrs. Shaw then wrote the words, "The heavy iron bells." Poe immediately completed the stanza which now reads:

Hear the tolling of the bells,—
Iron bells!
What a world of solemn thought their monody compels!
In the silence of the night,
How we shiver with affright
At the melancholy menace of their tone!
For every sound that floats
From the rust within their throats
Is a groan.
And the people—ah, the people—
They that dwell up in the steeple,
All alone,
And who tolling, tolling, tolling,
In that muffled monotone,
Feel a glory in so rolling
On the human heart a stone!
They are neither man nor woman,—
They are neither brute nor human,—
They are Ghouls;
And their king it is who tolls,—
And he rolls, rolls, rolls,
Rolls a pæan from the bells!
And his merry bosom swells
With the pæan of the bells!
And he dances, and he yells,
Keeping time, time, time,

In a sort of Runic rhyme,
To the pæan of the bells,
Of the bells.

The other stanzas were written afterward.
There is music in these words; but do not think
that the music is all. Underneath is the deep
harmony of human suggestion, as in the lines,

Feel a glory in so rolling
On the human heart a stone.

Now let us see if we can represent by musical
notes the meter in which this poem is written. We
must remember that a punctuation mark at the
end of a line often makes a complete pause, which
is represented in music by a rest. In music a rest
has the same effect in completing a bar as the cor-
responding note. Here are the first two lines:

Hear the sledg-es with the bells, Sil-ver bells!

In the two following lines the commas in the
middle of the line stand for rests, like the punctuation at the end of the first line; or if we wish we

can make the words "time, time, time," three longer notes. It all depends on how we pronounce them:

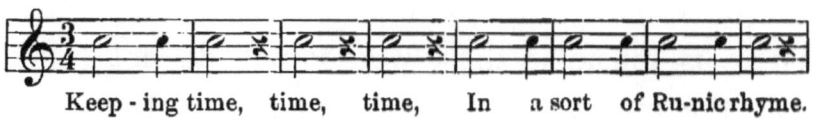

Keep - ing time, time, time, In a sort of Ru-nic rhyme.

CHAPTER XIII

POE'S LATER YEARS

Poe had the hardest time of his life when he was at New York, living in that little cottage at Fordham, where his poor wife died. He was always borrowing money, from sheer necessity, to keep himself and his wife from starvation. Once while in New York he was so hard pressed that Mrs. Clemm went out to see if she could not get work for him. She went to the office of Nathaniel P. Willis, who was the editor and proprietor of *The Mirror*. Willis was then starting *The Evening Mirror*, and said he would give Poe work. So the poet came; he had his little desk in the corner, and did his work meekly and regularly,—poor hack work for which he was paid very little.

Later he had an interest in a paper called *The Broadway Journal.* When it was about to cease publication Poe bought it himself for fifty dollars, giving a note which Horace Greeley endorsed and finally paid.

Once a young man wrote to Greeley, saying, "Doubtless among your papers you have many autographs of the poet, Edgar Allan Poe," and intimated that he should like to have one of them. Greeley wrote back that he had just one autograph of Poe among his papers; it was attached to a note for fifty dollars, and Greeley's own signature was across the back. The young man might have it for just half its face value.

But after Poe bought *The Broadway Journal* he had no money to carry it on, and its publication was soon suspended.

He earned his livelihood mainly by writing stories or articles for various magazines and papers, which paid him from $5 to $50 each. It was a hand to mouth way of living, for he was often, often disappointed.

In 1845, a volume entitled, ''Tales. By Edgar A. Poe,'' was published by Wiley and Putnam, and in the same year ''The Raven and Other Poems'' appeared in book form from the same publishing house. Poe also delivered lectures, and by way of criticism carried on what was called the ''Longfellow War.'' Though he considered Longfellow the greatest American poet, he accused him of plagiarism, or stealing some of his ideas, which was very unjust on the part of Poe. Hawthorne and Lowell he praised highly.

After the death of his wife, Poe was very melancholy. He went to lecture, and to visit friends in Providence, Rhode Island, and in Lowell, Massachusetts, and afterward went south to Richmond, where he planned to raise enough money by lecturing to start *The Stylus.*

He was hospitably entertained in Richmond, and became engaged to marry his boyhood's first love, Miss Royster, now the widow, Mrs. Shelton. Their marriage was to take place at once, and Poe started north to close up his business in New York and bring Mrs. Clemm south. In Baltimore it seems that he fell in with some politicians who were conducting an election. They took him about from one polling place to another to vote illegally; then some one drugged him, and left him on a bench near a saloon. Here he was found by a printer, who notified his friends, and they sent him to the hospital, where he died on the 7th of October, 1849. He was nearly forty-one years old.

Poe had a great and wonderful mind. In the latter part of his life he gave much of his time to a book called "Eureka," which was intended to explain the meaning of the universe. Of course he was not a philosopher; but he wrote some things in that book which were destined afterward to be accepted by such great men as Darwin and Huxley and many others.

His life was so full of work and poverty, so crossed and crossed again by unhappiness and hardship, that he never had time or strength of mind to think out anything as he would otherwise have done. All his work is fragmentary, broken bits on this subject or on that.   He wrote very few poems, not many stories, and only a little serious criticism.

But a Frenchman will tell you that Poe, among American poets and writers, is the greatest; his writings have been translated into nearly every European language.   In England, too, he is spoken of as our one great poet and critic, our first great story-writer, the inventor of the artistic short story.

Poor, unhappy Poe !   After his death a monument was to have been erected over his grave ; but by a strange fatality it was destroyed before it was finished.   Twenty-five years later admiring friends placed over his remains the first monument to an American poet.   No such memorial was needed, however, for American hearts will never cease to thrill at the weird, beautiful music of "Annabel Lee," "The Bells," and "The Raven."

THE STORY OF

JAMES RUSSELL LOWELL

JAMES RUSSELL LOWELL.

JAMES RUSSELL LOWELL

CHAPTER I

ELMWOOD

James Russell Lowell was born on the 22d of February, 1819, in Cambridge, Massachusetts. Elmwood, the home of the Lowells, was to the west of the village of Cambridge, quite near Mount Auburn cemetery. When James Russell was a boy, Elmwood was practically in the country, and was surrounded on nearly all sides by woods, meadows, and pastures. The house stood on a triangular piece of land surrounded by a very high and thick hedge, made up of all sorts of trees and shrubs, such as pines, spruces, willows, and oaks, with smaller shrubs at the bottom so as to form a thick wall of green. In front of the house were some fine English elms, quite different from the American variety, and from these the house got its name. It was a large, square, old-fashioned wooden house, and though it had stood for over a hundred years, it remained during Lowell's life in perfect condition.

The house was surrounded by a fine, well-kept lawn, and at the back were pasture, orchard, and garden, while half a mile away lay Fresh Pond, the haunt of herons and other shy birds and land creatures. From the upper windows one could look out on beautiful Mount Auburn cemetery, which was to the south, while to the east was a low hill called Symonds's Hill, beyond which could be seen a bright stretch of the Charles River.

Elmwood faced on a lane, between two roads. In his essay in "Fireside Travels," entitled "Cambridge Thirty Years Ago," Lowell describes the scene towards the village as it was in his childhood. Approaching "from the west, by what was then called the New Road (it is called so no longer, for we change our names whenever we can, to the great detriment of all historical association), you would pause on the brow of Symonds's Hill to enjoy a view singularly soothing and placid. In front of you lay the town, tufted with elms, lin-

dens, and horse-chestnuts. . . . Over it rose
the noisy belfry of the college, the square brown
tower of the church, and the slim yellow spire of
the parish meeting-house, by no means ungraceful,
and then an invariable characteristic of New England religious architecture. On your right the
Charles slipped smoothly through green and purple salt meadows, darkened here and there with
the blossoming black grass as with a stranded
cloud-shadow. Over these marshes, level as water
but without its glare, and with softer and more
soothing gradations of perspective, the eye was
carried to a horizon of softly rounded hills. To
your left upon the Old Road you saw some half
dozen dignified old houses of the colonial time, all
comfortably fronting southward." One of these,
the largest and most stately, was the Craigie
House, famous as the headquarters of Washington
in 1776, and afterwards as the home of Longfel·
low. And at the end of the New Road toward
Cambridge was a row of six fine willows, which had
remained from the stockade built in early days as
a defense against the Indians.

And here is Harvard Square, where stand the buildings of the famous college:

"A few houses, chiefly old, stood around the bare Common, with ample elbow-room, and old women, capped and spectacled, still peered through the same windows from which they had watched Lord Percy's artillery rumble by to Lexington, or caught a glimpse of the handsome Virginia general who had come to wield our homespun Saxon chivalry. People still lived who regretted the unhappy separation from the mother island. . . . The hooks were to be seen from which swung the hammocks of Burgoyne's captive redcoats. If memory does not deceive me, women still washed clothes in the town spring, clear as that of Bandusia. Commencement had not ceased to be the great holiday of the Puritan Commonwealth, and a fitting one it was—the festival of Santa Scholastica, whose triumphal path one may conceive strewn with leaves of spelling-books instead of bay."

James was the youngest of four brothers and two sisters, a handsome boy, and his mother's darling. He always thought he inherited his love of nature and poetic aspirations from her, whose family was from the Orkneys—those islands at the extreme north of Scotland.

His father was a strikingly handsome man, gracious and of rare personal qualities, and a faithful pastor over his flock. Often he took his youngest son on long drives with him, when he went to exchange pulpits with neighboring clergymen. Because of his wide family connection, and his father's position, James saw not a little of New England society as it was in those days, pure Yankee through and through.

CHAPTER II

AN IMPETUOUS YOUNG MAN

Young James was sent first to a dame school, as a private school for very small children kept by a lady in her own house was called in those days. But when he was eight or nine he was sent to a boarding school near Elmwood—going, of course, only as a day scholar. This school was kept by an

Englishman named Wells, who had belonged to a publishing firm in Boston which had failed. This teacher was very sharp and severe, but he made all his boys learn Latin, as you may see by reading the learned notes and introductions to the "Biglow Papers," supposed to have been written by "Parson Wilbur," but in reality by Lowell himself.

We sometimes find it difficult to believe that a great man whom we admire was ever an ordinary human being, with faults and errors like our own. But when we do find natural, childish letters, or read anecdotes of youthful naughtiness, we immediately feel like shaking hands with the scapegrace, and a real liking for him begins.

Lowell was so reserved in after life, and so very correct and elegant both in his writing and in his deportment, that when we come across two letters written at about nine years of age, badly punctuated and badly spelled, but displaying all the natural spirits of a boy, we begin at once to feel at home with him and to have a genuine affection for the man we had before only admired as a very great and learned author. Here are the two letters just as they were written. It will be a good exercise for you to rewrite them, correcting the spelling, punctuation, and other faults.

Jan. 25, 1827.

My dear brother The dog and the colt went down to-day with our boy for me and the colt went before and then the horse and slay and dog—I went to a party and I danced a great deal and was very happy—I read french stories—The colt plays very much—and follows the horse when it is out.

Your affectionate brother,
James R. Lowell.

I forgot to tell you that sister mary has not given me any present but I have got three books

Nov. 2, 1828.

My Dear Brother,—I am now going to tell you melancholy news. I have got the ague together with a gumbile. I presume you know that September has got a lame leg, but he grows better every day and now is very well but limps a little. We have a new scholar from round hill. his name is Hooper and we expect another named Penn who I believe also comes from there. The boys are all very well except Nemaise, who has got another piece of glass in his leg and is waiting for the doctor to take it out, and Samuel Storrow is also sick. I am going to have a new suit of blue broadcloth clothes to wear every day and to play in. Mother tells me I may have any sort of buttons I choose. I have not done anything to the hut, but if you wish I will. I am now very happy; but I should be more so if you were there. I hope you will answer my letter if you do not I shall write you no more letters. when you write my letters you must direct them all to me and not write half to mother as generally do. Mother has given me the three volumes of tales of a grandfather

farewell
Yours truly
James R. Lowell.

You must excuse me for making so many mistakes. You must keep what I have told you about my new clothes a secret if you dont I shall not divulge any more secrets to you. I have got quite a library. The Master has not taken his rattan out since the vacation. Your little kitten is as well and as playful as ever and I hope you are to for I am sure I love you as well as ever. Why

is grass like a mouse you cant guess that he he
he ho ho ho ha ha ha hum hum hum.

Young Lowell's life was so very quiet and un-
eventful that we have very little account of his
boyhood and youth. We know, however, that he
was fond of books and was rather lazy, and did
pretty much as he pleased. A poem which in
later years he dedicated to his friend Charles Eliot
Norton gives a very good picture of the life at
Elmwood:

The wind is roistering out of doors,
My windows shake and my chimney roars;
My Elmwood chimneys seem crooning to me,
As of old, in their moody, minor key,
And out of the past the hoarse wind blows,
As I sit in my arm-chair and toast my toes.

"Ho! ho! nine-and-forty," they seem to sing,
"We saw you a little toddling thing.
We knew you child and youth and man,
A wonderful fellow to dream and plan,
With a great thing always to come,—who knows?
Well, well! 't is some comfort to toast one's toes.

"How many times have you sat at gaze
Till the mouldering fire forgot to blaze,
Shaping among the whimsical coals
Fancies and figures and shining goals!
What matters the ashes that cover those?
While hickory lasts you can toast your toes.

"O dream-ship builder! where are they all,
Your grand three-deckers, deep-chested and tall,
That should crush the waves under canvas piles,
And anchor at last by the Fortunate Isles?
There's gray in your beard, the years turn foes,
While you muse in your arm-chair and toast your toes."

I sit and dream that I hear, as of yore,
My Elmwood chimneys' deep-throated roar;
If much be gone, there is much remains;
By the embers of loss I count my gains,
You and yours with the best, till the old hope glows
In the fanciful flame as I toast my toes.

Lowell entered Harvard College when he was
but fifteen years old, very nearly the youngest
man in his class. In those days the college was
small, there were few teachers, and only about
fifty students in a class.

CHAPTER III

COLLEGE AND THE MUSES

Soon after he entered college, young Lowell made the acquaintance of a senior, W. H. Shackford, to whom many of his published letters of college life are addressed. Another intimate friend was George Bailey Loring, who afterward became distinguished in politics. To one or other of these men he was constantly writing of his literary ambitions, always uppermost in his mind.

Josiah Quincy was president of Harvard when Lowell was there, and afterward Lowell wrote an essay on "A Great Public Character," which describes this distinguished president. In it he refers to college life in a way that shows he thoroughly enjoyed it.

"Almost every one," he writes, "looks back regretfully to the days of some Consul Plancus. Never were eyes so bright, never had wine so much wit and good-fellowship in it, never were we ourselves so capable of the various great things we have never done. . . . This is especially true of college life, when we first assume the titles without the responsibilities of manhood, and the president of our year is apt to become our Plancus very early."

In another of his essays he tells one of the standing college jokes, which is worth repeating. The students would go into one of the grocery stores of the town, whose proprietor was familiarly called "The Deacon."

"Have you any sour apples, Deacon?" the first student to enter would ask.

"Well, no, I haven't any just now that are exactly sour," he would answer; "but there's the bellflower apple, and folks that like a sour apple generally like that."

Enter the second student. "Have you any sweet apples, Deacon?"

"Well, no, I haven't any now that are exactly sweet; but there's the bellflower apple, and folks that like a sweet apple generally like that."

"There is not even a tradition of any one's ever having turned the wary Deacon's flank," says

Lowell, ''and his Laodicean apples persisted to
the end, neither one thing nor another.''

It did not take young Lowell long to find out
that he had a weakness for poetry (as his seniors
sometimes spoke of it). Writing to his friend
Loring, probably at the beginning of the Christmas
vacation, 1836, he says, ''Here I am alone in
Bob's room with a blazing fire, in an atmosphere of
'poesy' and soft coal smoke. Pope, Dante, a few
of the older English poets, Byron, and last, not
least, some of my own compositions, lie around
me. Mark my modesty. I don't put myself in the
same line with the rest, you see. . . . Been
quite 'grouty' all the vacation, 'black as Erebus.'
Discovered two points of very striking resemblance
between myself and Lord Byron; and if you will
put me in mind of it, I will propound next term,
or in some other letter, 'Vanity, thy name is
Lowell!'''

And again, in a letter to his mother, he says, ''I
am engaged in several poetic effusions, one of
which I dedicated to you, who have always been
the patron and encourager of my youthful muse.

If you wish to see me as much as I do you, I shall be satisfied."

This is Mrs. Lowell's answer to the last wish. She and Dr. Lowell were then making a visit to Europe: "Babie Jamie: Your poetry was very pleasing to me, and I am glad to have a letter, but not to remind me of you, for you are seldom long out of my head. . . . Don't leave your whistling, which used to cheer me so much. I frequently listen to it here, though far from you." In later years Lowell would often tell how he used to whistle as he came near home from school, in order to let his mother know he was coming, and she seldom failed to be sitting at her window to welcome him.

Early in 1837 Lowell was elected to the Hasty Pudding Club. "At the very first meeting I attended," he writes to his friend, Shackford, "I was chosen secretary, which is considered the most honorable office in the club, as the records are kept in *verse* (*mind*, I do not say *poetry*). This first brought my rhyming powers into notice, and since that I have been chosen to deliver the next anniversary poem by a vote of twenty out of twenty-four."

Not long afterward he writes to his friend Loring, "I have written about a hundred lines of my poem (?), and I suspect it is going to be pretty good. At least, some parts of it will take." And after a few lines he goes on, "I am as busy as a bee—almost. I study and read and write all the time." A little later he writes a letter to Loring in Scotch dialect verse.

This was not the sort of work, however, that the college authorities expected of him. He was lazy and got behind his classes, so that near the end of his course he was rusticated, or suspended from college for some weeks. He had been chosen class poet, but on account of his suspension he could not read his poem, though it was printed.

He was sent to Concord during this interval to carry on his studies under the minister of the town. Here he found it pretty dull, though Emerson and Thoreau were there. But he did not then care for either one of them. In one of his letters he said, "I feel like a fool. I must go down and see

Emerson and if he doesn't make me feel more like one, it won't be for want of sympathy. He is a good-natured man in spite of his doctrines."

Of Thoreau he said, "I met (him) last night, and it is exquisitely amusing to see how he imitates Emerson's tone and manner. With my eyes shut I shouldn't know them apart."

In the autumn he came back to Cambridge and took his degree of Bachelor of Arts with his class.

CHAPTER IV

HOW LOWELL STUDIED LAW

While at Concord, Lowell wrote to his friend Loring, as though explaining himself.

"Everybody almost is calling me 'indolent.' 'Blind dependent on my own powers' and 'on fate.' Confound everybody! since everybody confounds me. Everybody seems to see but one side of my character, and that the worst. As for my dependence on my own powers, 'tis all fudge. As for fate, I believe that in every man's breast are the stars of his fortune, which, if he choose, he may rule as easily as does the child the mimic constellations in the orrery he plays with. I acknowledge, too, that I have been something of a dreamer, and have sacrificed, perchance, too assiduously on that altar to the 'unknown God,' which the Divinity has builded not with hands in the bosom of every decent man, sometimes blazing out clear with flame, like Abel's sacrifice, heaven-seeking; sometimes smothered with greenwood and earthward, like that of Cain. Lazy quota! I haven't dug, 'tis true, but I have done as well, and 'since my free soul was mistress of her choice, and could of books distinguish her election,' I have chosen what reading I pleased and what friends I pleased, sometimes scholars and sometimes not."

Once out of college he had to take up some profession. Had poetry been a profession, he would have taken that; but such a choice at that time would have been considered sheer folly. He did not consider that he had any "call" to be a minister, still less a doctor. As there was nothing else left, he began the study of law. It is truly amusing to see how he manages to "wriggle along" until he takes his degree of LL. B. and is admitted to the bar.

First, he announces that he is "reading Blackstone with as good a grace and as few wry faces as he may." Only a few days later he declares, "A very great change has come o'er the spirit of my dreams. I have renounced the law." He is going to be a business man, and sets about looking for a place in a store. He is going to give up all thoughts of literary pursuits and devote himself to money-making. He also says, "I have been thinking seriously of the ministry, but then—I have also thought of medicine, but then—still worse!"

A few days pass by. He goes into Boston and hears Webster speak in a case before the United States Court. "I had not been there an hour before I determined to continue in my profession and study as well as I could."

Still, it was hard work to keep at his law studies. He is soon writing to his friend George Loring, "I sometimes think that I have it in me, and shall one day do somewhat ; meantime I am schooling myself and shaping my theory of poesy."

Six weeks later: "I have written a great deal of *pottery* lately. I have quitted the law forever." Then he inquires if he can make any money by lecturing at Andover. He already has an engagement to lecture at Concord, where he has hopes to "astonish them a little."

A fortnight later we find him in a "miserable state. The more I think of business the more really unhappy do I feel, and think more and more of studying law." What he really wants to do all the time is to write poetry. "I don't know how it is," he says, "but sometimes I actually *need* to write somewhat in verse." Sunday is his work day in the "pottery business."

As for the law, it is settled at last. He writes to his friend, "Rejoice with me, for to-morrow I shall be free. Without saying a word to any one, I shall quietly proceed to Dane Law College to recitation. Now shall I be happy again as far as that is concerned."

A fortnight later he declares, "I begin to like

the law, and therefore it is quite interesting. I am determined that I *will* like it and therefore I *do*."

In the summer of 1840 he completed his studies and was admitted to the bar. A little later he opened an office in Boston. Misfortune had overtaken his father, and his personal property had been nearly swept away. It was now necessary for the young man to earn his own living. His friends were therefore glad that he had his profession to depend on.

CHAPTER V

LOVE AND LETTERS

Lowell always had a presentiment that he should never practice law. He was always dreaming of becoming independent in some other way. "Above all things," he declares, "should I love to sit down and do something literary for the rest of my natural life."

He did not then think of marrying, and it does

not require much to support a single man. Though he opened a law office in Boston, it does not appear that he did any business. He wrote a story entitled - "My First Client," but one of his biographers unkindly suggests that this may have been purely imaginary.

All through his letters we see his ambitious yearning. "George," says he in one place, "before I die your heart shall be gladdened by seeing your wayward, vain, and too often selfish friend do something that shall make his name honored. As Sheridan once said, 'It's *in* me, and' (we'll skip the oath) 'it shall come *out!*'"

His bachelor dreams were soon dissipated, however. He went to visit a friend of his, W. A. White, and there met the young man's sister Maria. He thought her a very pleasant and pleasing young lady, and he discovered that she knew a great deal of poetry. She could repeat more verse than any other one of his acquaintances, though he laments that she was more familiar with modern poets than with the "pure wellsprings of English poesy."

The friendship grew apace. In the same fall that he began the pretended practice of law he became engaged to her, and she caused a fresh and voluminous outpouring of verse. His productions were printed in various periodicals, such as the *Knickerbocker Magazine*, to which Longfellow had contributed, and the *Southern Literary Messenger*, which Poe once edited.

Miss White was a most charming and interesting young lady. She was herself a poet, and had a delicate intellectual sympathy that enabled her to enter into her lover's ambitions, and assist him even in the minutest details of his work.

It is fair to suppose that Lowell's friends brought every possible pressure to bear upon him to make him give up poetry and *dig* at the law. His father's financial losses had left him without an inherited income; he was engaged to a beautiful girl and anxious to be married; in some way he must earn his living, and if possible do more. Such was not the effect, however. He devoted himself to poetry with an almost feverish activity. He has made up his mind that he will do something great; for only so can he hope possibly to make literature a paying profession. ·

It was Maria who inspired most of his verse at this time. One of his best poems even to this day was written directly for her. It is called "Irené." It may be taken as the best possible description of his lady herself:

> Hers is a spirit deep, and crystal-clear;
>   Calm beneath her earnest face it lies,
> Free without boldness, meek without a fear,
>   Quicker to look than speak its sympathies;
> Far down into her large and patient eyes
>   I gaze, deep-drinking of the infinite,
> As, in the mid-watch of a clear, still night,
>   I look into the fathomless blue skies.

As the struggle between money and law on the one side and literature on the other still went on, he expressed his feelings on the subject to his friend Loring in the following stanza, which puts the whole argument into a nutshell:

> They tell me I must study law.
> They say that I have dreamed and dreamed too long,
>   That I must rouse and seek for fame and gold;
> That I must scorn this idle gift of song,

And mingle with the vain and proud and cold.
Is, then, this petty strife
The end and aim of life,
All that is worth the living for below?
O God! then call me hence, for I would gladly go!

Thus he had finally come to the conclusion that he would rather die than give up literature.

"Irené" won the good opinion of many. The young poet, though but twenty-one, felt that he was beginning to be a lion. His next definite step was to publish a volume of verses. Says he, "I shall print my volume. Maria wishes me to do it; and that is enough."

So his first volume, "A Year's Life," was published, with the motto in German, "I have lived and loved."

The young poet's friends were very much opposed to this publication, for the reason that a rising young lawyer is not helped on in his profession at all by being known as a poet. Who would employ a *poet* to defend his business in a court room? No one! A hard-headed business man is wanted. Walter Scott was a lawyer of much such a temperament as Lowell's, and when he put forth a similar volume he suffered as it was certain that Lowell would suffer. But it is probable that Lowell was now fully determined to give up law altogether.

"I know," he declares passionately, "that God has given me powers such as are not given to all, and I will not 'hide my talent in mean clay.' I do not care what others may think of me or of my book, because if I am worth anything I shall one day show it. I do not fear criticism as much as I love truth. Nay, I do not fear it at all. In short, I am happy. Maria fills my ideal and I satisfy her. And I mean to live as one beloved by such a woman should live. She is every way noble. People have called 'Irené' a beautiful piece of poetry. And so it is. It owes all its beauty to her."

It is very plain that she was on the side of the poet, not of the worldly-minded persons who advocated the law, business, money-making. She did not dread the prospect of being a poor man's wife. To be the wife of a poet, a man of courage and

ambition and nobleness of heart, was far more to
her. The turning point in Lowell's life was past;
and he had been led to that turning point by the
little woman who was soon to become his wife.

CHAPTER VI

THE UNCERTAIN SEAS OF LITERATURE

As far as is known, Lowell never earned a dollar
by the law. He soon began to pick up a five or a
ten dollar bill here and there by writing for current
periodicals. His book brought him some reputation, but not much. A few hundred copies were
sold, and most of the reviews and criticisms were
favorable. He received a slating from the *Morning Post* in Boston, however, just as an inkling of
what a literary man might expect.

Three years of hard literary work now followed.
Lowell wrote assiduously and heroically, getting
what happiness he could in the meantime out of
his love. He was young and strong, and life was
not a burden. He tells us of having spent an

evening at the house of a friend "where Maria is making sunshine just now," and he declared that he had been exceedingly funny. He had in the course of the evening recited "near upon five hundred extempore macaronic verses; composed and executed an oratorio and opera" upon a piano without strings, namely the center-table ; drawn "an entirely original view of Nantasket Beach" ; made a temperance address ; and given vent to "innumerable jests, jokes, puns, oddities, quiddities and nothings," interrupted by his own laughter and that of his hearers. Besides this, he had eaten "an indefinite number of raisins, chestnuts (!), etc., etc., etc., etc., etc."

In 1842 Lowell and Cobert G. Carter, who was about the same sort of a business man as the poet himself, started a periodical which they called the *Pioneer*. They had no capital ; but they did have literary connections, and they were able to get together for the three numbers they published a larger number of contributions from distinguished contributors than has often fallen to the lot of any American periodical. It is true that these men were not as famous in those days as they have since become ; still, their names were known and their reputations were rapidly growing. The best known were Poe, Hawthorne, Longfellow, Whittier and Emerson ; but there were not a few others whose names are well known to-day. The magazine had a high literary character, and was well worthy of the future greatness of the contributors. Unfortunately, it takes something more than literary excellence to make a successful magazine. Sometimes the literary quality is too high for the public to appreciate. This was true of the *Pioneer*. A magazine also requires a large capital and commercial ability in the business office. It is not at all strange that the venture did not succeed. It could not have done so. Three numbers only were issued, and those three left behind them a debt which the young publishers were unable to pay until some time after.

At the same time that Lowell was having trouble with his magazine, he found his eyes becoming affected, and he was obliged to spend the greater part of the winter of 1842-43 in New York to undergo treatment. Here he made many new literary acquaintances, among others that of Charles F. Briggs, who started the *Broadway Journal* with the assistance of Poe. In the meantime, he kept on writing poetry with more vigor than ever, and in 1843 published a second volume of verse, containing his best work since "A Year's Life" appeared.

His contributions to the periodicals included much prose as well as poetry. Among other things, he wrote a series of "Conversations on some of the Old Poets," which was published in a volume the same year that the second book of poems came out. It consisted mainly of essays on Chaucer, Chapman, Ford, and the old dramatists. He never cared to reprint this first excursion into the realm of literary criticism ; but it opened up a field which he was to work with distinction in after years.

Lowell's prose is delicate, airy, and fanciful, but at the same time keenly critical and sharp in its thought. "Fireside Travels" and "From My Study Window" are books which are known all over the world and which are everywhere voted "delightful."

CHAPTER VII

HOSEA BIGLOW, YANKEE HUMORIST

In December, 1844, Lowell felt that his income from his literary work, though very small and precarious, was sufficient to justify him in marrying, and accordingly he was united to Miss White. She was delicate in health, and after their marriage the couple went to Philadelphia, where they spent the winter in lodgings. Lowell became a regular contributor to the *Freeman,* an antislavery paper once edited by Whittier. From this he derived a very small but steady income; and the next year he was engaged to write every week for the *Anti-Slavery Standard* on a yearly salary of five hundred dollars. This connection he maintained for the next four years.

In June, 1846, the editor of the *Boston Courier,* a weekly paper well known in the "Hub" for its literary character even to this day, received a strange communication. It was a letter signed "Ezekiel Biglow," enclosing a poem written by his son Hosea. This is the way the letter began:

Jaylem, june, 1846.

Mister Eddyter:—Our Hosea wuz down to Boston last week, and he see a cruetin Sarjunt a struttin round as popler as a hen with 1 chicking, with 2 fellers a drummin and fifin arter him like all nater, the sarjunt he thout Hosea hed n't gut his i teeth cut cos he looked a kindo's though he 'd jest cum down, so he cal'lated to hook him in, but Hosy wood n't take none o his sarse for all he hed much as 20 Rooster's tales stuck onto his hat and eenamost enuf brass a bobbin up and down on his shoulders and figureed onto his coat and trousis, let alone wut nater hed sot in his featers, to make a 6 pounder out on.

The letter was rather a long one, and closed thus. Referring to the verses enclosed, the writer says:—

If you print em I wish you 'd jest let folks know who hosy's father is, cos my ant Kesiah used to say it 's nater to be curus ses she, she aint livin though and he 's a likely kind o lad.

Ezekiel Biglow.

The poem itself began with this stanza:
Thrash away, you 'll *hev* to rattle
On them kittle-drums o' yourn,—

'Taint a knowin' kind o' cattle
  Thet is ketched with mouldy corn;
Put in stiff, you fifer feller,
  Let folks see how spry you be,—
Guess you 'll toot till you are yeller
  'Fore you git ahold o' me!

The letter and the poem were printed together in the *Courier*, and immediately were the talk of the town. You will remember that in 1846 the war with Mexico was just beginning, and many people were opposed to it as the work of "jingo" politicians, controlled in some degree by the slavery power. Southern slaveholders wished to increase the territory of the United States in such a way as to enlarge the territory where slavery would be lawful. The antislavery people of New England were violently opposed to the war, and this poem by the Yankee Hosea Biglow immediately became popular, because it put in a humorous, common-sense way what everybody else had been saying with deadly earnest.

Charles Sumner saw the common sense of the poem, but did n't see the fun in the bad spelling. Said he, "This Yankee poet has the true spirit.

He puts the case admirably. I wish, however, he could have used good English." Evidently Sumner did not suspect that so cultured and polished a poet as James Russell Lowell was the author of a stanza like this:

> 'Wut 's the use o' meetin'-goin'
>   Every Sabbath, wet or dry,
> Ef it 's right to go amowin'
>   Feller-men like oats and rye?
> I dunno but wut it 's pooty
>   Trainin' round in bobtail coats.—
> But it 's curus Christian dooty,
>   This 'ere cuttin' folks's throats.

The fact is, however, Lowell had written all this, even the letter with bad spelling purporting to come from Ezekiel Biglow. He was deeply interested in the antislavery cause, in good politics and sound principles; yet he saw that it would be useless for him to get up and preach against what he did not like. There were plenty of other earnest, serious-minded men like Garrison and Whittier who were fighting against the evil in the straightforward, blunt way. Lowell was as interested as they in having the wrongs righted; but he was more cool-headed than the rest. He considered the matter. A joke, he said to himself, will carry the crowd ten times as quickly as a serious protest; and people will listen to one of their own number, a common, every-day, sensible fellow with a spark of wit in him, where they would go away bored by polished and cultured writing full of Latin quotations. This is how he came to begin the Biglow papers. Their instant success proved that he was quite right.

Of course it was not long before shrewd people began to see that this fine humor, with its home-thrusts, was not in reality written by a country bumpkin. Through the rough dialect and homely way of stating the case, there shone the fine intellect of a cultivated and skillful writer. The *Post* guessed that James Russell Lowell was the real author. This was regarded only as a rumor, however, and many people scouted the idea that a young poet, whose books sold only in small numbers and were known only to literary people, could have written anything as good as this.

" I have heard it demonstrated in the pauses of

a concert," wrote Lowell afterward, "that I was utterly incompetent to have written anything of the kind."

It was early in this same summer of 1846 that Lowell made his contract to write regularly for the *Anti-Slavery Standard;* and he soon began sending the "Biglow" poems to that paper instead of to the *Courier*.

The most popular of the whole series of poems by Hosea Biglow was the one on John P. Robinson. Robinson was a worthy gentleman who happened to come out publicly on the side of a political wire-puller. Immediately Hosea caught up his name and wrote a comic poem on voting for a bad candidate for office. Looked at in that light, the poem applies just as well to political candidates to-day as it did then. Here are a few stanzas of the poem. You will want to turn to "Lowell's Poetical Works" and read the whole piece.

WHAT MR. ROBINSON THINKS.

Guvener B. is a sensible man;
   He stays to his home an' looks arter his folks;
He draws his furrer ez straight ez he can,

An' into nobody's tater-patch pokes;
 But John P.
 Robinson he
 Sez he wunt vote fer Guvener B.

My! aint it terrible ? Wut shall we du ?
 We can't never choose him o' course—thet's flat;
Guess we shall hev to come round, (don't you?)
 An' go in fer thunder an' guns, an' all that,
 Fer John P.
 Robinson he
 Sez he wunt vote fer Guvener B.

Gineral C. is a dreffle smart man:
 He's ben on all sides thet give places or pelf;
But consistency still wuz a part of his plan—
 He's been true to *one* party—an' thet is himself;
 So John P.
 Robinson he
 Sez he shall vote fer Gineral C.

Gineral C. he goes in fer the war;
 He don't vally principle more'n an old cud;
Wut did God make us raytional creeturs fer,
 But glory an' gunpowder, plunder an' blood ?
 So John P.
 Robinson he
 Sez he shall vote fer Gineral C.

The side of our country must ollers be took,
 An' President Polk, you know, *he* is our country.

An' the angel that writes all our sins in a book
  Puts the *debit* to him, an' to us the *per contry;*
    And John P.
    Robinson he
    Sez this is his view o' the thing to a T.

There is a story that Mr. Robinson couldn't go anywhere after this poem was published without hearing some one humming or reciting,

    Fer John P.
    Robinson he
    Sez he wunt vote fer Guvener B.

School children shouted it everywhere, people on the street repeated it as they met, and the funny rhyme was heard even in polite drawing-rooms, amid roars of laughter. Mr. Robinson went abroad, but scarcely had he landed in Liverpool before he heard a child crooning over to himself,

    Fer John P.
    Robinson he
    Sez he wunt vote fer Guvener B.

In Genoa, Italy, it was a parody, telling what John P.—Robinson he— would do down in Judee.

CHAPTER VIII

PARSON WILBUR

In the course of time the "Biglow Papers" were published in book form. Not only was Lowell's name not yet connected publicly with the Yankee humor, but the poems were provided with an elaborate introduction, notes and comments, by the learned pastor of the church at Jaalam, Homer Wilbur. His notes and introduction are filled with Latin quotations, and he appears as much a scholar as Hosea Biglow does a natural. He says he tried to teach Hosea better English, but decided to let him work out his own ideas in his own way. Still, he endorses Hosea's principles, and is in every way thoroughly his friend.

This Parson Wilbur is almost as much of a character in the book as Hosea himself, and his prose, printed at the beginning and end of each poem in small type, is almost as clear and effective and interesting as Hosea's poems. We are always tempted to skip anything printed in small type, and placed in brackets; but in this case that would be a great mistake.

Speaking of "What Mr. Robinson Thinks," Parson Wilbur says, "A bad principle is comparatively harmless while it continues to be an abstraction, nor can the general mind comprehend it fully till it is printed in that large type which all men can read at sight, namely the life and character, the sayings and doings, of particular persons. . . .

"Meanwhile, let us not forget that the aim of the true satirist is not to be severe upon persons, but only upon falsehood, and as Truth and Falsehood start from the same point, and sometimes even go along together for a little way, his business is to follow the path of the latter after it diverges, and to show her floundering in the bog at the end of it. Truth is quite beyond the reach of satire. There is so brave a simplicity in her, that she can no more be made ridiculous than an oak or a pine. The danger of the satirist is, that continual use may deaden his sensibility to the force of language. He becomes more and more liable to strike harder than he knows or intends. He may put on his boxing gloves, and yet forget that the older they grow, the more plainly may the knuckles inside be felt. Moreover, in the heat of contest, the eye is insensibly drawn to the crown of victory, whose tawdry tinsel glitters through the dust of the ring which obscures Truth's wreath of simple leaves."

There is another very interesting passage which is said to be an extract from one of the Parson's sermons, describing the modern newspaper.

"Wonderful, to him that has eyes to see it rightly, is the newspaper. To me, for example, sitting on the critical front bench of the pit, in my study here in Jaalam, the advent of my weekly journal is as that of a strolling theater, or rather of a puppet-show, on whose stage, narrow as it is, the tragedy, comedy, and farce of life are played in little. Behold the huge earth sent to me hebdom- idally in a brown paper wrapper."

You see that what he says is very learned in its choice of words ; but if you read it carefully you will find it interesting.

But after all, Parson Wilbur is a humorous character, though he has his sense, too. At the end of his introduction are some fragmentary notes which are intended as a general satire on editors of books. He goes on at some length to say that he thought he ought to have his picture printed in the book which he professes to be editing. But he has only two likenesses, one a black profile, the other a painting in which he is made cross-eyed. He speaks of it as ''strabismus,'' which sounds very learned of course, and he goes on to explain that in actual fact this is not a bad thing, for he can preach very directly at his congregation, and no one will think the preacher has him particularly in his eye. He also says Mrs. Wilbur objected to having a cross-eyed picture reproduced, and he is therefore driven to take the position of those great people who refuse to have their features copied at all. Then he puts in a lot of absurd genealogical notes.

At the beginning of the book there are also a number of imaginary notices of ''the independent press.'' Of course there are no such papers as those mentioned, and the praise and the blame are alike satirical.

In the original volume of "Biglow Papers," part of a page at the end of these "Notices of the Press" remained unfilled, and the printer asked Lowell if he could not send in something to occupy that space. As poetry came easiest, Lowell wrote a number of stanzas about "Zekle's Courtin'." There were only six stanzas in the original edition. Lowell wrote more, but told the printer to break off when the page was filled. This the printer did, and the stanzas which were not put in type were lost, as Lowell had kept no copy. This piece became so popular that friends urged the poet to finish the story, and he wrote a few more stanzas. Then he wrote still others. In the course of time it developed into the long poem printed with the second series of "Biglow Papers," under the title of "The Courtin'."

This is the way it runs in the first version; but you will want to read it also in its complete form:

Zekle crep' up quite unbeknown,
  An' peeked in thru the winder,
An' there sot Huldy all alone,
  'ith no one nigh to hender.

He kin' o' l'itered on the mat,
  Some doubtfle o' the sekle,
His heart kep' goin' pitypat,
  But hern went pity Zekle.

He stood a spell on one foot fust,
  Then stood a spell on tother,
An' on which one he felt the wust
  He could n't ha' told ye, nuther.

Sez he, "I'd better call agin;"
  Sez she, "Think likely, *Mister;*"
The last word pricked him like a pin,
  An'—wal, he up and kist her.

When in the course of the publication of the
second series of "Biglow Papers," twenty years
after the first, it was announced that Parson Wilbur
was dead, people who had read the first series felt
very much as though they had lost a personal
friend. The public had learned to love the pe-
dantic, vain old man as if he were a real human
being. Lowell had created in him a great character of fiction, almost as if he were a novelist instead of a poet.

CHAPTER IX

A FABLE FOR CRITICS

Lowell's next attempt in the satirical and humorous line was a long poem written somewhat after the style of the old Latin fable writers, and hence called "A Fable for Critics." It was written in double rhymes, for the most part, which are very hard to make, and not altogether easy to read; but they help the humorous impression.

This poem was published anonymously, and in it the author hits off all the prominent authors of the day, speaking as the god Apollo. Of course he did not attach his name to it, and as it appeared anonymously he felt that he could say what he liked—in other words, tell the truth about his friends and acquaintances, or at least give his opinion of them. Incidentally, he pokes fun at the literary fads of the day.

Among other things, to give the impression that he was not the author of the poem, he puts in a free criticism of himself:

There is Lowell, who 's striving Parnassus to climb
With a whole bale of *isms* tied together with rhyme.
He might get on alone, spite of brambles and boulders,
But he can't with that bundle he has on his shoulders.
The top of the hill he will never come nigh reaching
Till he learns the distinction 'twixt singing and preaching;
His lyre has some chords that would ring pretty well,
But he 'd rather by half make a drum of the shell,
And rattle away till he 's old as Mathusalem,
At the head of a march to the last new Jerusalem.

Evidently he thought that he paid too much attention to politics, as in the ''Biglow Papers,'' and to lecturing, and various side issues, when he ought to be cultivating pure poetry more assiduously; or rather, he would have liked to be a simple poet and do nothing else, not even earn a living.

The way he characterizes in this poem the great writers whom we know is both amusing and interesting, and he generally tells the truth. For instance, he writes—

There comes Poe, with his raven, like Barnaby Rudge,
Three fifths of him genius and two fifths sheer fudge.

The best of his criticisms are not satirical, but true and appreciative. Thus, Hawthorne:

There is Hawthorne, with genius so shrinking and rare
That you hardly at first see the strength that is there;
A frame so robust, with a nature so sweet,
So earnest, so graceful, so lithe, and so fleet,
Is worth a descent from Olympus to meet.

His reference to Whittier, too, is a noble tribute by one poet to another:

There is Whittier, whose swelling and vehement heart
Strains the strait-breasted drab of the Quaker apart,
And reveals the live Man, still supreme and erect,
Underneath the bemummying wrappers of sect.

Bryant was the oldest of the American poets, and the generation to which Lowell belonged had been taught to look up to him as the head of American poetical literature. Of course the younger poets felt that they ought to receive a share of the homage, and perhaps they were a little jealous of Bryant.

There is Bryant, as quiet, as cool, and as dignified,
As a smooth, silent iceberg that never is ignified,
Save when by reflection 't is kindled o' nights
With a semblance of flame by the chill Northern Lights.

This is not at all complimentary, it would seem,

but a little farther along Lowell makes up for it in
part by saying—

But, my dear little bardlings, don't prick up your ears,
Nor suppose I would rank you and Bryant as peers;
If I call him an iceberg I don't mean to say,
There is nothing in that which is grand in its way;
He is almost the one of your poets that knows
How much grace, strength, and dignity lie in Repose.

You will remember that in one of his college letters, written while he was at Concord because
rusticated, Lowell did not seem to care for Emerson.   He afterward became his great admirer,
and in this fable leads off with Emerson, saying:

There comes Emerson first, whose rich words, every one,
Are like gold nails in temples to hang trophies on,
Whose prose is grand verse, while his verse, the Lord
    knows,
Is some of it pr—No, 't is not even prose.

Irving and Holmes are two more of his favorites.
Of the first he says:

What! Irving ? Thrice welcome, warm heart and fine
    brain,
You bring back the happiest spirit from Spain,
And the gravest sweet humor, that ever were there
Since Cervantes met death in his gentle despair.

Holmes he happily hits off thus:

There's Holmes, who is matchless among you for wit;
A Leyden jar always full charged, from which flit
The electrical tingles of hit after hit.
His are just the fine hands, too, to weave you a lyric
Full of fancy, fun, feeling, or spiced with satiric;
In a measure so kindly, you doubt if the toes
That are trodden upon are your own or your foe's.

And he ends by saying:

Nature fits all her children with something to do;
He who would write and can't write, can surely review,
Can set up a small booth as critic and sell us his
Petty conceit and his pettier jealousies.

Lowell was a good critic, and clearly saw the merit of the really great writers of his time. We have quoted his characterizations of those he admires. His keen thrusts at those who are not half as great as they would have us believe are both amusing and true, and no doubt made their victims smart sharply enough, for instance that—

One person whose portrait just gave the least hint
Its original had a most horrible squint.

CHAPTER X

THE TRUEST POETRY

While Lowell was becoming famous indirectly as the anonymous author of the "Biglow Papers" and "A Fable for Critics," he was writing and publishing over his own name sweet, simple lines that came straight from his heart and which will no doubt be remembered when the uncouth Yankee dialect of Hosea Biglow and the hard rhymes of the "Fable" are forgotten. The simpler a true poet is the more beautiful and really poetic he is likely to be. The simplest thing Lowell ever wrote was "The First Snow-Fall," composed in 1847 after the death of his little daughter Blanche, with the sorrow for whose loss was mingled the joy at the coming of another child.

THE FIRST SNOW-FALL.

The snow had begun in the gloaming,
    And busily all the night
Had been heaping field and highway
    With a silence deep and white.

I stood and watched by the window
  The noiseless work of the sky,
And the sudden flurries of snow-birds,
  Like brown leaves whirling by.

I thought of a mound in sweet Auburn
  Where a little headstone stood;
How the flakes were folding it gently,
  As did robins the babes in the wood.

Up spoke our own little Mabel,
  Saying, "Father, who makes it snow?"
And I told of the good All-father
  Who cares for us here below.

Again I looked at the snow-fall,
  And thought of the leaden sky
That arched o'er our first great sorrow,
  When that mound was heaped so high.

I remembered the gradual patience
  That fell from that cloud like snow,
Flake by flake, healing and hiding
  The scar that renewed our woe.

And again to the child I whispered,
  " The snow that husheth all,
Darling, the merciful Father
  Alone can make it fall!"

Then with eyes that saw not, I kissed her;
  And she, kissing back, could not know
That my kiss was given to her sister,
  Folded close under deepening snow.

Lowell's greatest poem, "The Vision of Sir Launfal," was written in the same simple, beautiful spirit of "The First Snow-Fall," and that is why we all like to read it over and over again. "Sir Launfal" was a favorite with Mrs. Lowell from the beginning. She probably knew better that it was a great poem than the poet himself did.

The "Prelude" to the first part is beautiful because it contains so much that cannot but touch the heart of every one, however he may dislike poetry. A great poem like this cannot be read hastily, nor must we stop with reading it once. Great poetry must be read so many times that it is committed entirely to memory before we begin to reach the end of the beauties in it. Each time we reread we see new beauties, we feel new thrills.

> Over his keys the musing organist,
>   Beginning doubtfully and far away,
> First lets his fingers wander as they list,
>   And builds a bridge from Dreamland for his lay;
> Then, as the touch of his loved instrument
>   Gives hope and fervor, nearer draws his theme,
> First guessed by faint auroral flashes sent
>   Along the wavering vista of his dream.

The first time you read this passage it may mean little to you; but as you read again and again you gradually picture in your mind a grand cathedral, just filling with people for the morning worship. The organist begins with a few light notes, fanciful, merely suggestive; then louder and louder swells the strain; the music begins to bring up before your mind pictures of waterfalls, cities, men and women with passionate hearts; at last, in the grand flood of the music, you forget yourself, the world around you, the church, the thronging congregation, everything.

After this pretty and suggestive prelude, describing the musician, we read such passages as this, which suggest the theme as by a "faint auroral flash":

> And what is so rare as a day in June?
> Then, if ever, come perfect days;
> Then Heaven tries earth if it be in tune,
> And over it softly her warm ear lays.

A little farther along the music seems to broaden and deepen:

Now is the high-tide of the year,
  And whatever of life hath ebbed away
Comes flooding back with a ripply cheer,
  Into every bare inlet and creek and bay;
Now the heart is so full that a drop overfills it,
We are happy now because God wills it.

You must read the rest of the poem for yourself, ever remembering that to read poetry so that you understand it and love it means that you yourself are a poet at heart; and if you come to love a great poem you may be proud of your achievement.

CHAPTER XI

PROFESSOR, EDITOR, AND DIPLOMAT

There was a touching and very warm affection between Longfellow and Lowell. Mrs. Lowell says of it, "I have never seen such a beautiful friendship between men of such distinct personalities, though closely linked together by mutual tastes and affections. They criticise and praise each other's performances with frankness not to be surpassed, and seem to have attained that happy height of faith where no misunderstanding, no jealousy, no reserve exists." Often in his diary Longfellow speaks of ''walking to see Lowell,''who was either ''musing before his fire in his study,'' or occupied in his '' celestial study, with its pleasant prospect through the small square windows.''

Longfellow was some dozen years the elder; and when the time came that he wished to retire from the professorship of belles-lettres in Harvard College, he was very desirous that Lowell should take the place. There were others who wanted it; but it was arranged that Lowell should become Longfellow's successor. Lowell had never before been a professor and he did not particularly like the work. In 1867 he speaks of ''beginning my annual dissatisfaction of lecturing next week.'' Still, he was popular with the students and highly successful because of his fine gift of literary criticism. Here, for instance, is his definition of poetry: ''Poetry, as I understand it, is the recognition of something new and true in thought or feeling, the recollection of some profound experience, the conception of some heroic action, the creation of something beautiful and pathetic."

In his diary Longfellow sometimes refers to Mrs. Lowell, "slender and pale as a lily"; and once when he and Charles Sumner had gone to see Lowell and found that he was not at home, Longfellow adds, "but we saw his gentle wife, who, I fear, is not long for this world."

His words were prophetic. She gradually failed in strength. Of their four children, three died while mere babes. In 1853 Mrs. Lowell herself died.

The appointment to Longfellow's professorship did not come until a little over a year after the death of Mrs. Lowell. During her life Mr. Lowell's income was very small and irregular, a few hundred dollars a year in payment of royalties on his books and for articles and poems contributed to various periodicals. With his appointment to the Harvard professorship he became financially independent for the first time. To prepare for it he went abroad, spending most of his time at Dresden.

He returned sooner than he expected, and for a reason that very well illustrates his business habits. When he set out he had a limited amount of money. This he placed with London bankers, arranging to draw on them for such sums as he might need from time to time. He asked that when he had drawn down to a certain sum the bankers should notify him, and then he would immediately prepare to return home. He settled down, and thought that he was getting on moderately well and had a considerable sum still to draw. What was his surprise when he was notified by his bankers that he had drawn his account down to the amount he had mentioned! As there was nothing better for him to do, he packed his trunk and went home.

Some years after that, he received a letter from these London bankers informing him that an error had been made in his account, and that a draft for a hundred pounds sterling (five hundred dollars) which had been drawn by some other person named Lowell had by mistake been charged to his account. This money, with compound interest, was now at his disposal. The bankers suggested, however, that if he was not in immediate need of the money, they would use it for an admirable investment they knew of which might considerably increase it within a year. At the end of a year he received a draft for seven hundred pounds. This he used to refurnish Elmwood. "Now, you, who are always preaching figures and Poor Richard, and business habits," said he, in telling the story to some friends, "what do you say to that? If I had kept an account and known how it stood, *I should have spent that money* and you would not now be sitting in those easy chairs, or walking on Wilton carpet. No; hang accounts and figures!"

In 1857 the *Atlantic Monthly* was started, and Lowell was made editor, with a salary of three thousand dollars a year, of course in addition to his salary as a Harvard professor. Though he was the editor, he recognized that the success of the magazine would be made by Holmes. Said he, "You see, the doctor is like a bright mountain stream that has been dammed up among the hills and is waiting for an outlet into the Atlantic. You will find that he has a wonderful store of thought —serious, comic, pathetic, and poetic,—of comparisons, figures, and illustrations. I have seen nothing of his preparation, but I imagine he is ready. It will be something wholly new, and his reputation as a prose writer will date from this magazine." When you recollect the success of the "Autocrat of the Breakfast Table" you cannot help remarking that Lowell was a veritable prophet.

President Hayes, soon after his inauguration, offered Lowell an appointment as minister to Austria, but Lowell declined. When he was asked if he would accept an appointment as minister to Spain, he consented, and thither he went in the early part of President Hayes' administration. After a time he was transferred to London, where he became a striking diplomatic figure.

He was one of the most popular and polished gentlemen ever sent as ambassador to a European nation, and as such his presence at the Court of Saint James was highly appreciated by the English people. When, in 1884, on the election of Cleveland to the presidency, he prepared to leave London, many glowing tributes were paid him by the English press, but none was more hearty than this, printed in *Punch:*

Send you away? No, Lowell, no.
 That phrase, indeed, is scarce well chosen.
We're glad, of course, to have you go
 More like a brother than a cousin ;
True, we must "speed the parting guest,"
 If such a guest from us *must* sever;
But what we all should like the best
 Would be to keep you here forever.

You've won our hearts; your words, your ways,
 Are what we like. Without desiring
To sicken you with fulsome praise,
 We think you've seen no signs of tiring.
Of graceful speech, of pleasant lore,
 How much to you the English mind owes!
We're sad to think we'll see no more
 Of you—save through your Study Windows.

Well, well, the best of friends must part;
 That's commonplace, like Gray, but true, sir.
Commend us to the Yankee heart;
 If you can come again, why, *do*, sir.
What Biglow calls our "English sarse,"
 Is not *all* tarts and bitters, is it?
Farewell!—if from us you must pass,
 But try, *do* try, another visit!

After his return from England, Mr. Lowell did comparatively little literary work. Some years before this, he had married the lady who was educating his only daughter. He now spent the most of his time at Elmwood among his books and in the society of his friends. In 1888 a volume of his later poems appeared, bearing the title of ''Heartsease and Rue.'' About the same time '' Democracy,'' a collection of the addresses which he had delivered in England, was published. But neither of these volumes added materially to his fame.

On the twelfth of August, 1891, the famous poet, essayist, and man of affairs died. He was nearly seventy-three years of age.

NOTE.—The thanks of the publishers are due Messrs. Harper & Brothers for permission to use extracts from '' Letters of James Russell Lowell, edited by Charles Eliot Norton,'' and to Messrs. Houghton, Mifflin & Co. for permission to use extracts from the Poetical Works of Lowell.

THE STORY OF
BAYARD TAYLOR

BAYARD TAYLOR.

BAYARD TAYLOR

CHAPTER I

HIS BIRTH AND CHILDHOOD

Bayard Taylor was born in the country village of Kennett Square, Chester County, Pennsylvania, Jan. 11, 1825, "the year when the first locomotive successfully performed its trial trip. I am, therefore," he says, "just as old as the railroad." He was descended from Robert Taylor, a rich Friend, or Quaker, who had come to Pennsylvania with William Penn in 1681, and settled near Brandywine Creek. Bayard's grandfather married a Lutheran of pure German blood, and on that account was expelled from the Society of Friends, which at that time had very strict rules regarding the marriage of its members. Although the family still used the peculiar speech of the Quakers, and clung to the Quaker principles of peace and order, none of them ever returned to the society.

When Bayard was four years old, the family moved to a farm about a mile from the village. There they lived, until, years afterward, the successful traveler and poet bought an estate near by and built a magnificent house upon it, into which he received his father and mother and brothers and sisters, with that open-hearted generosity and hospitality which was so much a part of his nature.

He was the fourth child of his parents; but the three older children had died in infancy, and he remained as the eldest of the family.

Chester County, Pennsylvania, has always been a rich farming region, peopled by solid, well-to-do farmers, many of whom are Quakers. Here the northern elms toss their arms to the southern cypresses, as the poet has it; the two climates seem to meet and mingle, in a sort of calm, neutral zone, and the vegetation of the North is united with the vegetation of the South, to produce a peculiar richness and variety.

In such surroundings the boy grew up, a farmer's lad, and learned that love of nature which was a part of his being till the day he died. "The child," says he, ''that has tumbled into a newly plowed furrow never forgets the smell of the fresh earth. . . . Almost my first recollection is of a swamp, into which I went barelegged at morning, and out of which I came, when driven by hunger, with long stockings of black mud, and a mask of the same. If the child was missed from the house, the first thing that suggested itself was to climb upon a mound which overlooked the swamp. Somewhere among the tufts of rushes and the bladed leaves of the calamus, a little brown ball was sure to be seen moving, now dipping out of sight, now rising again, like a bit of drift on the rippling green. It was my head. The treasures I there collected were black terrapins with orange spots, baby frogs the size of a chestnut, thrush's eggs, and stems of purple phlox."

He loved his home with a passionate intensity; but he also had yearnings for the unknown world beyond the horizon. "I remember," says he, ''as distinctly as if it were yesterday the first time this passion was gratified. Looking out of the garret window, on a bright May morning, I discovered a row of slats which had been nailed over the shingles for the convenience of the carpenters in roofing the house, and had not been removed. Here was, at least, a chance to reach the comb of the steep roof, and take my first look abroad into the world! Not without some trepidation I ventured out, and was soon seated astride of the sharp ridge. Unknown forests, new fields and houses, appeared to my triumphant view. The prospect, though it did not extend more than four miles in any direction, was boundless. Away in the northwest, glimmering through the trees, was a white object, probably the front of a distant barn; but I shouted to the astonished servant girl, who had just discovered me from the garden below, 'I see the Falls of Niagara!'"

He was a sensitive child and had a horror of dirty hands, "and," says he, "my first employments—picking stones and weeding corn—were rather a torture to this superfine taste." In his mother, however, he had a friend who understood and protected him. So his life on the farm was as happy as it well could be, in spite of its roughness. He himself has described it with a zest which no one else could lend it. "Almost every field had its walnut tree, melons were planted among the corn, and the meadow which lay between never exhausted its store of wonders. Besides, there were eggs to hide at Easter; cherries and straw-berries in May; fruit all summer; fishing parties by torchlight; lobelia and sumac to be gathered, dried and sold for pocket money; and in the fall, chestnuts, persimmons, wild grapes, cider, and the grand butchering after frost came, so that all the pleasures I knew were incidental to a farmer's life. The books I read came from the village library, and the task of helping to 'fodder' on the dark winter evenings was lightened by the anticipation of sitting down to 'Gibbon's Rome' or 'Thaddeus of Warsaw' afterwards."

He was fond of reading, and especially fond of poetry, and his wife in her biography says: "In the evening after he had gone to bed, his mother would hear him repeating poem after poem to his brother, who slept in the same room with him."

CHAPTER II

SCHOOL LIFE

Bayard had the advantage of regular attendance at the country schools near his father's home, with two or three years at the local academy; but his father could not afford to send him to college. He enjoyed his school life, and in after years wrote to one of his early Quaker teachers thus:

"I have never forgotten the days I spent in the little log schoolhouse and the chestnut grove behind it, and I have always thought that some of the poetry I then copied from thy manuscript books has kept an influence over all my life since. There was one verse in particular which has cheered and encouraged me a thousand times when prospects seemed rather gloomy. It ran thus:

'O, why should we seek to anticipate sorrow
    By throwing the flowers of the present away,
And gathering the dark-rolling, cloudy to-morrow
    To darken the generous sun of to-day?'

Thou seest I have good reason to remember those old times, and to be grateful to thee for encouraging instead of checking the first developments of my mind."

You may easily guess from this letter that Bayard's school life was very sedate and Quakerish. Nearly all the people in Kennett Square were Quakers, and though Bayard's father and mother were not, they had all the Quaker habits. Among other things, he was taught the wickedness of all kinds of swearing. His mother "talked so earnestly on this point that his mind became full of it; his observation and imagination were centered upon oaths, until at last he was so fascinated that he became filled with an uncontrollable desire to swear. So he went out into a field, beyond hearing, and there delivered himself of all the oaths he had ever heard or could invent, and in as loud a voice as possible." After this he felt quite satisfied to swear no more.

When Bayard was about twelve years old, his father was elected sheriff of the county and went to live at West Chester for three years. The young lad was sent to Bolmar's Academy at that place; and when the family went back to the farm he was sent to the academy at Unionville, three or four miles from his home. Here, at the age of sixteen, he finished his regular schooling. During the last two years he studied Latin and French, and during the last year Spanish. His Latin and French he continued by private study for three years longer.

He now went back to work on the farm for a season, and, as he says, "first felt the delight and refreshment of labor in the open air. I was then able to take the plow handle, and I still remember the pride I felt when my furrows were pronounced even and well turned. Although it was already decided that I should not make farming the business of my life, I thrust into my plans a slender wedge of hope that I might one day own a bit of ground, for the luxury of having, if not the profit of cultivating, it. The aroma of the sweet soil had tinctured my blood; the black mud of the swamp still stuck to my feet."

After a few weeks of farm life he was apprenticed to a printer in West Chester for a term of four years.

CHAPTER III

HIS FIRST POEM

It is the will and the spirit that makes every life seem happy or the reverse. If Bayard Taylor had remained a farmer in Kennett Square all his life, he would not have looked back on his early experiences with so much pleasure as he did. Indeed, we may safely say that he would not have liked his life so well at the time had it not been for his buoyant and hopeful nature, which made him feel that he was destined for higher and better things, for a world beyond the horizon.

Already he was a poet, with all a poet's aspirations and eagerness. A year before he left the academy his first printed poem appeared in the *Saturday Evening Post* of Philadelphia. It is not wonderful as poetry. Yet we read it with interest, because it shows so plainly the earnest and ambitious, yet cheerful, nature of the boy. He did not merely sit and hope; he was determined to *win his way*. It is entitled, "Soliloquy of a Young Poet."

A dream!— a fleeting dream!
Childhood has passed, with all its joy and song,
And my life's frail bark on youth's impetuous stream
        Is swiftly borne along.

High hopes spring up within;
Hopes of the future—thoughts of glory—fame,
Which prompt my mind to toil, and bid me win
        That dream—a deathless name.

        *   *   *   *

I know it all is vain,
That earthly honors ever must decay,
That all the laurels bought by toil and pain
        Must pass with earth away.

But still my spirit high,
Longing for fame won by the immortal mind—
On fancy's pinion fain would scale the sky,
        And leave dull earth behind.

Yes, I would write my name
With the star's burning ray on heaven's broad scroll,
That I might still the restless thirst for fame
        Which fills my soul.

Bayard Taylor was not a great genius, and he did not succeed in winning quite all of that high fame for which he struggled throughout his life. He never expected to have earth's blessings

showered upon him without working for them; and
the fact that he failed somewhat in his highest
ambition—to be a far-famed poet—makes his life
seem nearer to our own. We call him a great
man because he did well what came to him to do,
working hard all his life. In this we can all follow
his example.

CHAPTER IV

SELF-EDUCATION AND AMBITION

"The Village Record" (to the proprietor of
which Bayard was apprenticed) was printed upon
an old-fashioned hand press, and it was the business of the apprentices to set the type, help make
up the paper, pull the forms, and send the weekly
issues off to the subscribers.

The mechanical work was soon learned, and the
young apprentice found considerable time for reading. He now began that work of self-education
which he carried on through his whole life.
Already, before he left the academy, he had

become acquainted with the works of Charles
Dickens, and had secured the great man's autograph. "I went to the Academy," says he,
"where I received a letter that had come on Saturday. It was from Hartford; I knew instantly it
was from Dickens. It was double, and sealed
neatly with a seal bearing the initials C. D. In
the inside was a sheet of satin notepaper, on which
was written, 'Faithfully yours, Charles Dickens,
City Hotel, Hartford, Feb. 10, 1842'; and below,
'with the compliments of Mr. Dickens.' I can
long recollect the thrill of pleasure I experienced
on seeing the autograph of one whose writings I so
ardently admired, and to whom, in spirit, I felt
myself attached ; and it was not without a feeling
of ambition that I looked upon it that as he, a
humble clerk, had risen to be the guest of a mighty
nation, so I, a humble pedagogue [he was then
pupil teacher at the Academy], might by unre-
mitted and arduous intellectual and moral exertion
become a light, a star, among the names of my
country. May it be !"

When he went to work at West Chester his

reading was chiefly poetry and travel. The result of his "fireside travels" we shall soon see. The way in which he read poetry may be gathered from the following extract from a letter to one of his comrades :

"By the way, what do you think of Bryant as a poet, and especially of 'Thanatopsis'? For my part, my admiration knows no bounds. There is an all-pervading love of nature, a calm and quiet but still deep sense of everything beautiful. And then the high and lofty feeling which mingles with the whole ! It seems to me when I read his poetry that our hearts are united, and that I can feel every throb of his answered back by mine. This is what makes a poet immortal. There are but few who make me feel so thrillingly their glowing thoughts as Bryant, Longfellow, Whittier, and Lowell (all Americans, you know), and these I *love*. It is strange, the sway a master mind has over those who have felt his power."

Another poet of whom he was an enthusiastic admirer was Tennyson. He had read a criticism by Poe. "I still remember," he wrote afterward, "the eagerness with which as a boy of seventeen, after reading his paper, I sought for the volume; and I remember also the strange sense of mental dazzle and bewilderment I experienced on the first perusal of it. I can only compare it to the first sight of a sunlit landscape through a prism; every object has a rainbow outline. One is fascinated to look again and again, though the eyes ache."

He contributed several poems to the *Saturday Evening Post*, and then wrote to Rufus W. Griswold, who, besides being connected with the *Post*, was the editor of *Graham's Magazine*, the leading literary periodical at that time. Those of us who know the life of Poe remember Griswold as the man who pretended to be his friend, but who after Poe's death wrote his life, filling it with all the scandalous falsehoods he could hear of or invent. To Bayard Taylor, however, he seems to have been a helpful friend.

"I have met with strange things since I wrote last," writes Taylor to a school friend in March, 1843. "Last November I wrote to Mr. Griswold, sending a poem to be inserted in the *Post*. However, I said that it was my highest ambition to appear in *Graham's Magazine.* Some time ago I got an answer. He said he had read my lines 'To the Brandywine,' which appeared in the *Post*, with much pleasure, and would have put them in the magazine if he had seen them in time. He said the poem I sent him would appear in April in the magazine, and requested me to contribute often and to call on him when I came to town. I never was more surprised in my life."

He went to Philadelphia the next autumn, and consulted Griswold regarding a poetic romance he had written—about a thousand lines in length—and Griswold advised him to publish it in a volume with other poems. He wrote to a friend to inquire how much the printing and binding would cost, and finding that the expense would not be very great, he concluded to ask his friends to subscribe for the volume. When he had received enough subscriptions to pay the cost of publication, he brought the volume out. It was entitled "Ximena; or, The Battle of the Sierra Morena, and Other Poems. By James Bayard Taylor." (The James was added by mistake by Griswold.) It was dedicated "To Rufus W. Griswold, as an expression of gratitude for the kind encouragement he has shown the author."

The poems contained in this volume were never republished in after years. The book was fairly successful, and was distinctly a step upward; but it did not fill the young writer with undue conceit. In writing to a friend of his ambition at this time, he says: "It is useless to deny that I have cherished hopes of occupying at some future day a respectable station among our country's poets. I believe all poets are possessed in a greater or less degree of ambition; it is inseparable from the nature of poetry. And though I may be mistaken, I think this ambition is never given without a mind of sufficient power to sustain it, and to achieve its lofty object. Although I am desirous of the world's honors, yet with all the sincerity I possess I declare that my highest hope is to do good; to raise the hopes of the desponding; to soothe the sorrows of the afflicted. I believe that poetry owns as its true sphere the happiness of mankind."

What could be nobler and more sensible than that! Even his earliest poetry has in it no false, slipshod sentiment. Its subject is nature and heroic incident, and is indeed a faithful attempt to carry out the aim so well stated above. Some have doubted whether Bayard Taylor really had the power which he says he thinks is given to all who have the ambition which he felt. But none can fail to admire the spirit in which he worked, and to feel satisfied with the results, whatever they may be.

CHAPTER V

A TRAVELER AT NINETEEN

It was not as a poet, however, that Bayard Taylor was to win his first fame. At the age of nineteen, when he had but half completed his four years' term of apprenticeship, he made up his mind to go to Europe. He had no money; but that did not appear to him an insurmountable obstacle. He thought he could work his way by writing letters for the newspapers. So he went up to Philadelphia and visited all the editors. For three days he went about; but all in vain. The editors gave him little encouragement. He was on the point of going home, but with no thought of giving up his project.

At last two different editors offered him each fifty dollars in advance for twelve letters, and the proprietor of *Graham's Magazine* paid him forty dollars for some poems. So he went back to Kennett Square the jubilant possessor of a hundred and forty dollars.

He succeeded in buying his release from the articles of apprenticeship, and immediately prepared to set out on foot for New York, where he and two others were to take ship for England. That was the beginning of a career of travel which lasted many years, and brought him both fame and money.

In a delightful essay on "The First Journey I Ever Made," he says that while other great travelers have felt in childhood an inborn propensity to go out into the world to see the regions

beyond, he had the intensest desire to climb upward—so that without shifting his horizon, he
could yet extend it, and take in a far wider sweep
of vision. "I envied every bird," he goes on,
"that sat singing on the topmost bough of the
great, century-old cherry tree; the weathercock on
our barn seemed to me to whirl in a higher region
of the air; and to rise from the earth in a balloon
was a bliss which I would almost have given my
life to enjoy." His desire to ascend soon took the
practical form of wishing to climb a mountain.
By great economy he saved up fifteen dollars, and
with a companion who had twenty-seven dollars
(enormous wealth!) he set out for a walking tour
to the Catskills, with the hope of going even so far
as the Connecticut valley.

No doubt the feelings he experienced in setting
out on that excursion, at the end of his first year
as an apprentice, would apply equally well to the
greater journey he was to attempt a year later.

"The steamboat from Philadelphia deposited
me at Bordentown, on the forenoon of a warm,
clear day. I buckled on my knapsack, inquired

the road to Amboy, and struck off, resolutely, with
the feelings of an explorer on the threshold of great
discoveries. The sun shone brightly, the woods
were green, and the meadows were gay with phlox
and buttercups. Walking was the natural impulse
of the muscles; and the glorious visions which the
next few days would unfold to me, drew me on-
ward with a powerful fascination. Thus, mile after
mile went by; and early in the afternoon I reached
Hightstown, very hot and hungry, and a little foot-
sore. Twenty-five cents only had been expended
thus far—and was I now to dine for half a dollar?
The thought was banished as rapidly as it came,
and six cakes, of remarkable toughness and heavi-
ness, put an effectual stop to any further prompt-
ings of appetite that day.

"The miles now became longer, and the rosy
color of my anticipations faded a little. The sandy
level of the country fatigued my eyes; the only
novel objects I had yet discovered were the sweep-
poles of the wells. . . . The hot afternoon
was drawing to a close, and I was wearily looking
out for Spotswood, when a little incident occurred,

the memory of which has ever since been as re-
freshing to me as the act in itself was at the time.

"I stopped to get a drink from a well in front of
a neat little farmhouse. While I was awkwardly
preparing to let down the bucket, a kind, sweet
voice suddenly said: 'Let me do it for you.' I
looked up, and saw before me a girl of sixteen,
with blue eyes, wavy auburn hair, and slender
form—not strikingly handsome, but with a shy,
pretty face, which blushed the least bit in the
world, as she met my gaze.

"Without waiting for my answer, she seized
the pole and soon drew up the dripping bucket,
which she placed upon the curb. 'I will get
you a glass,' she then said, and darted into the
house—reappearing presently with a tumbler in
one hand and a plate of crisp tea-cakes in the
other. She stood beside me while I drank, and
then extended the plate with a gesture more invit-
ing than any words would have been. I had had
enough of cake for one day; but I took one, nevertheless, and put a second in my pocket, at her
kind persuasion.

"This was the first of many kindnesses which I have experienced from strangers all over the wide world; and there are few, if any, which I shall remember longer.

"At sunset I had walked about twenty-two miles, and had taken to the railroad track by way of change, when I came upon a freight train, which had stopped on account of some slight accident.

"'Where are you going?' inquired the engineer.

"'To Amboy.'

"'Take you there for a quarter!'

"It was too tempting; so I climbed upon the tender and rested my weary legs, while the pines and drifted sands flew by us an hour or more—and I had crossed New Jersey!"

This little description may be taken as a type of the way in which he traveled and the way in which he described his travels—a way that almost immediately made him famous, and caused the public to call for volume after volume from his pen.

CHAPTER VI

TWO YEARS IN EUROPE FOR FIVE HUNDRED DOLLARS

A journey to Europe was not the common thing in those days that it has since become, and no American had then thought of tramping over historic scenes with little or no money. So this journey, projected and carried out by Bayard Taylor, was really an original and daring undertaking. It was all the more remarkable from the fact that the people of the community where he had been born and brought up had scarcely ever gone farther from their homesteads than Philadelphia.

In New York he visited all the editors with an introduction from Nathaniel P. Willis; but none of them gave him any encouragement, except Horace Greeley, the famous editor of the *Tribune*. Here is Bayard Taylor's own description of the interview: "When I first called upon this gentleman, whose friendship it is now my pride to claim, he addressed me with that honest bluntness which is habitual to him: 'I am sick of descriptive letters, and will have no more of them. But I should like some sketches of German life and society, after you have been there and know something about it. If the letters are good, you shall be paid for them, but don't write until you know something.' This I faithfully promised, and kept my promise so well that I am afraid the eighteen letters which I afterward sent from Germany, and which were published in the *Tribune*, were dull in proportion as they were wise."

The journey was indeed to Taylor a serious thing. "It did not and does not seem like a pleasure excursion," he writes; "it is a duty, a necessity."

On the 1st of July, 1844, Taylor and his two companions embarked on the ship "Oxford," bound for Liverpool. They had taken a second-cabin passage, the second cabin being a small place amidships, flanked with bales of cotton and fitted with temporary and rough planks. They paid ten dollars each for the passage, but were obliged to find their own bedding and provisions. These latter the ship's cook would prepare for them for a small compensation. All expenses included, they found they could reach Liverpool for twenty-four dollars apiece.

At last they were actually afloat. "As the blue hills of Neversink faded away, and sank with the sun behind the ocean, and I felt the first swells of the Atlantic," he writes, "and the premonitions of seasickness, my heart failed me for the first and last time. The irrevocable step was taken; there was no possibility of retreat, and a vague sense of doubt and alarm possessed me. Had I known anything of the world, this feeling would have been more than momentary; but to my ignorance and enthusiasm all things seemed possible, and the thoughtless and happy confidence of youth soon returned."

The experiences of the next two years he has also told briefly and tersely. "After landing in Liverpool," he says, "I spent three weeks in a walk through Scotland and the north of England, and then traveled through Belgium, and up the Rhine ·to Heidelberg, where I arrived in September, 1844. The winter of 1844-45 I spent in

Frankfurt on the Main [in the family in which N. P. Willis's brother Richard was boarding], and by May I was so good a German that I was often not suspected of being a foreigner. I started off again on foot, a knapsack on my back, and visited the Brocken, Leipsic, Dresden, Prague, Vienna, Salzburg, and Munich, returning to Frankfurt in July. A further walk over the Alps and through Northern Italy took me to Florence, where I spent four months learning Italian. Thence I wandered, still on foot, to Rome and Civita Vecchia, where I bought a ticket as deck-passenger to Marseilles, and then tramped on to Paris through the cold winter rains. I arrived there in February, 1846, and returned to America after a stay of three months in Paris and London. I had been abroad two years, and had supported myself entirely during the whole time by my literary correspondence. The remuneration which I received was in all $500, and only by continual economy and occasional self-denial was I able to carry out my plan. I saw almost nothing of intelligent European society; my wanderings led me among the com-

mon people. But literature and art were nevertheless open to me, and a new day had dawned
in my life."

CHAPTER VII

THE HARDSHIP OF TRAMP TRAVEL

Making a journey without money, without know-
ing the language of the people, and without any
experience in travel is not at all the sort of thing
it seems to one who has not gone through its toils,
but only sees the glow and glamour of success.
We cannot pass on without giving some of the
details of commonplace hardship which Bayard
Taylor endured on this first European journey.

Taylor knew a little book French, but neither
he nor either of his companions could speak it or
understand it when spoken, and they knew nothing at all of German. When they reached Frankfurt they tried to inquire the way to the house of
the American consul. At first they were not at all
able to make themselves understood; but finally
they found a man who could speak a little French

and who told them that the consul resided in "Bellevue" street. It was in reality "Shone Aussicht," which is the German for beautiful view, as Bellevue is the French. But the young travelers knew nothing of this. They went in search of "Bellevue" street, and though they wandered over the greater part of the town and suburbs, they did not find it. At last they decided to try all the streets which had a beautiful view, and in this way soon found the consul's house.

Not only did they have very little money in any case, but they were frequently obliged to wait months for remittances. While in Italy, Taylor's funds ran so low, and he became so discouraged, that he gave up going to Greece, as he had at first planned. He was expecting a draft for a hundred dollars; but that would barely pay his debts. "My clothes," he writes to one of his companions, "are as bad as yours were when you got to Heidelberg, nearly dropping from me; and I cannot get them mended. What is worse, they must last till I get to Paris." Later he speaks of spending three dollars for a pair of trousers, as those he wore would not hold together any longer. In despair, he exclaims, "It is really a horrible condition. If there ever were any young men who made the tour of Europe under such difficulties and embarrassments as we, I should like to see them."

But all this only urged him to greater efforts. "I tell you what, Frank," he writes almost in his next letter, "I am getting a real rage in me to carve out my own fortune, and not a poor one, either. Sometimes I almost desire that difficulties should be thrown in my way, for the sake of the additional strength gained in surmounting them."

These words were written from Italy; but yet harder things were in store for him. "I reached London for the second time about the middle of March, 1846," he writes in his paper on "A Young Author's Life in London," "after a dismal walk through Normandy and a stormy passage across the Channel. I stood upon London Bridge, in the raw mist and the falling twilight, with a franc and a half in my pocket, and deliberated what I should do. Weak from sea-sickness, hungry, chilled, and without a single acquaintance in the great city, my situation was about as hopeless as it is possible to conceive. Successful authors in their libraries, sitting in cushioned chairs and dipping their pens into silver inkstands, may write about money with a beautiful scorn, and chant the praise of Poverty—the 'good goddess of Poverty,' as George Sand, making 50,000 francs a year, enthusiastically terms her;—but there is no condition in which the Real is so utterly at variance with the Ideal, as to be actually out of money, and hungry, with nothing to pawn and no friend to borrow from. Have you ever known it, my friend? If not, I could wish that you might have the experience for twenty-four hours, only once in your life."

On this occasion Bayard Taylor went to a chop-house where he could get a wretched bed for a shilling. The next morning he took a sixpenny breakfast, and started out to look for work. By good fortune he met Putnam, the American publisher, who lent him a sovereign (five dollars) and gave him work that would enable him to earn his living until he could get money from America for his return passage.

CHAPTER VIII

HIS FIRST LOVE AND GREATEST SORROW

At the very first school which Bayard Taylor attended there was a little Quaker girl who would whisper with a blush to her teacher, "May I sit beside Bayard?" Her name was Mary Agnew. As schoolmates and neighbors the two children grew up together; and in time Bayard began to confide to his diary his dream of happiness with her. Toward this object, all his thoughts and plans were gradually directed.

Mary Agnew's father did not countenance this neighbor lover, however, and when Bayard set out for Europe he was not allowed to write to her. He sent messages through his mother, and occasionally heard from the young girl in the same way. On his return, however, he grew more bold, and soon became openly engaged to her. The romance is a sadly beautiful one; for this fair girl who was his inspiration during the years of his hardest struggles, finally fell into a decline and died just as he was beginning to earn the money that would have made them happy together.

"I remember him," says a neighbor, speaking of the two at this time, "as a bright, blushing, diffident youth, just entering manhood; and with him I always associate that gentle and beautiful girl, with matchless eyes, who inspired many of his early lyrics, and whose death 'filled the nest of love with snow.'"

Mary Agnew reminds us of Poe's beautiful Virginia Clemm, his "Annabel Lee." Grace Greenwood wrote of her as "a dark-eyed young girl with the rose yet unblighted on cheek and lip, with soft brown, wavy hair, which, when blown by the wind, looked like the hair oft given to angels by the old masters, producing a sort of halo-like effect about a lovely head."

And Taylor at this time was evidently her match in looks as well as spirit. A German friend describes him thus : "He was a tall, slender, blooming young man, the very image of youthful beauty and purity. His intellectual head was sur-rounded by dark hair; the glance of his eyes was so modest, and yet so clear and lucid, that you seemed to look right into his heart."

On his return from Europe, young Taylor found that his letters to the newspapers had attracted some attention, perhaps largely owing to the fact that one who was almost a boy had made the journey on foot, with little or no money. At the same time he had told his story in a simple, straightforward way, which proved him to be a good reporter. Friends advised him to gather the letters into a volume, which he did under the title, "Views Afoot; or Europe Seen with Knap-sack and Staff." Within a year six editions were sold, and the sale continued large for a number of years.

Yet this success, quick as it was, did not solve all his difficulties at once. He was anxious to earn a good living as soon as possible, that he might marry Mary Agnew. After looking the field over, he and a friend bought a weekly paper published in Phœnixville, a lively manufacturing town in the same county as his home. This, with the aid of his friend, he edited and managed for a year. He not only failed to make money, but accumulated debts which he was three years in paying off. At the same time he found that he could no longer endure a narrow country life. He tried to give his paper a literary tone; but the people did not want a literary paper. They cared more for local news and gossip, which he hated.

The old ambition and aspiration to be and to do something really worth doing was still uppermost with him. In a letter to Mary Agnew he says: "Sometimes I feel as if there were a Providence watching over me, and as if an unseen and uncontrollable hand guided my actions. I have often dim, vague forebodings that an eventful destiny is in store for me; that I have vast duties yet to accomplish, and a wider sphere of action than that which I now occupy. These thoughts may be vain; they spring only from the ceaseless impulses of an upward-aspiring spirit; but if they *are* real, and to be fulfilled, I shall the more need thy love and the gladness of thy dear presence."

He wrote to his friends in New York about getting work there, but they did not encourage him much. Horace Greeley bluntly advised him to stay where he was. The editor of the *Literary World*, however, offered him employment at five dollars a week. He thereupon sold out his interest in his country paper at a loss, and went to try his fortunes in New York. Before he had been there many weeks, Horace Greeley offered him a position on the *Tribune* at twelve dollars a week. The connection thus begun lasted for the rest of his life. It was as the *Tribune's* correspondent that he traveled all over the world. He was soon able to buy stock in the *Tribune* company, and this was the foundation of his future fortune.

He had many literary and other distinguished friends in New York. And during these first few years he worked very hard indeed, hoping soon to earn enough money to provide for Mary Agnew. In 1850, after three years in New York, he was able to set the date of their marriage. But it was postponed from time to time on account of her illness. At last he knew that she could never be well again; yet in any case he wished the marriage ceremony performed. They were accordingly married October 24, 1850; and two months later she was dead.

CHAPTER IX

"THE GREAT AMERICAN TRAVELER"

It had been Bayard Taylor's boyhood ambition to become a great poet; but it seemed as if fate meant him for a great traveler. He was sorry that this was so: yet he was fond of travel, and never refused any opportunity to visit other lands. In 1849, when the California gold fever was at its height, he was sent by the *Tribune* to the Pacific Coast.

"I went," he says, "by way of the Isthmus of Panama — the route had just been opened — reached San Francisco in August, and spent five months in the midst of the rough, half-savage life of a new country. I lived almost entirely in the open air, sleeping on the ground with my saddle for a pillow, and sharing the hardships of the gold diggers, without taking part in their labors."

On his return he gathered his letters into a volume entitled "Eldorado, or Adventures in the Path of Empire: comprising a voyage to California, via Panama; Life in San Francisco and Monterey; Pictures of the Gold Region, and Experiences of Mexican Travel."

He now began to feel the strength and confidence of success; his brain was seething with new ideas, and he felt as if he could do that which would realize the destiny of which he had dreamed. But sorrow was already at his door. His hopes were for the time broken and thrown back by the death of Mary Agnew.

In the summer of 1851 he found himself worn out and depressed. His health was shattered and his mind was overpowered. But a change and rest were at hand. The editors of the *Tribune* suggested his going to Egypt and the Holy Land. In the autumn he set out, and spent the winter in ascending the Nile to Khartoum. He even went up the White Nile to the country of the Shillooks, a region then scarcely known to white men.

Bayard Taylor fancied that he had two natures, one a southern nature and one a northern nature. Of course the northern nature was his regular and ordinary one. In one of his later journeys, when he had entered Spain from France and was sitting down to a breakfast of red mullet and oranges fresh from the trees, "straightway," he says, " I took off my northern nature as a garment, folded it and packed it neatly away in my knapsack, and took out in its stead the light, beribboned and bespangled southern nature, which I had not worn for eight or nine years."

He donned this southern nature for the first time on his trip to California by way of Panama. Horace Greeley especially commended his letter from Panama. But it was during his journey in Egypt that he became most saturated with the south, and composed his " Poems of the Orient "— perhaps the best he ever wrote. He had not been in Alexandria a day and a half before he wrote to his mother that he had never known such a delicious climate. "The very air is a luxury to breathe," he said. "I am going to don the red cap and sash," he wrote from Cairo, "and sport a saber at my side. To-day I had my hair all cut within a quarter of an inch of the skin, and when I look in the glass I see a strange individual. Think of me as having no hair, a long beard, and a copper-colored face." So much like a native did he become that when he entered the bank in Constantinople for his letters and money, they addressed him in Turkish.

He made the journey up the Nile on a boat with a wealthy German landowner, a Mr. Bufleb, who became to him like a brother, though he was nearly twice the age of Taylor. Some years later the young man married Mrs. Bufleb's niece.

When he reached Constantinople he received a letter from the managers of the *Tribune* suggesting that he go across Asia to Hong-Kong, China, and join the expedition of Commodore Perry to Japan. As the expedition would not reach Hong-Kong for some months, however, he had time to visit his German friend and go on to London. From London he returned through Spain and went by way of the Suez, Bombay, and Calcutta to China, stopping on the way to view the Himalayas.

Commodore Perry made the young journalist "master's mate," and gave him a place on the flagship. This was necessary, because no one not a member of the navy was allowed to accompany the expedition.

There is not space to detail the wonderful sights he saw or the interesting experiences he had. He reached New York, December 20, 1853, after an absence of more than two years, and found that in his absence he had become almost famous. His letters in the *Tribune* had been read all over the country, and everybody wanted to know more of the "great American traveler."

He at once prepared for the press three books. They were "A Journey to Central Africa; or, Life and Landscapes from Egypt to the Negro Kingdoms of the Nile"; "The Land of the Saracens; or, Pictures of Palestine, Asia Minor, Sicily, and

Spain "; and "A Visit to India, China, and Japan in the Year 1853."

He had hundreds of calls to lecture; and thereafter for several years he made lecturing his principal business. From his books and his lectures he received large sums of money, so that before he was thirty he had accumulated a modest fortune.

In 1856 Bayard Taylor took his two sisters and his youngest brother to Europe. He left them in Germany, while he himself carried out a plan long in his mind, of visiting northern Sweden and Lapland in winter. The following summer he visited Norway, and later published the results of these journeys in "Northern Travel."

While in Germany, after his trip to Sweden, he became engaged to Marie Hansen, daughter of Prof. Peter A. Hansen, the noted astronomer and founder of Erfurt Observatory. They were married in the following autumn, October 27, 1857.

He now hurried home with his wife and prepared to build a house and lay out the country estate

which he called Cedarcroft. The land had belonged to one of his ancestors, and he was very
proud of his fine country house; but he found it
a rather expensive enjoyment.

CHAPTER X

HIS POETRY

We have seen how in youth Bayard Taylor con-
ceived the ambition to be known as one of his
country's great poets. He saw his books of travel
sell by the hundred thousand; but while this
brought him money and notoriety, he clung still to
his poetry. He even felt annoyed when he heard
himself spoken of as "the great American traveler"
instead of the great American poet. The truth is,
he had not been able to give to poetry the time or
energy he could have wished; and he afterwards.
worked with desperate energy to recover those
lost poetic opportunities.

Yet in his busiest days he was always writing

verses, which in the minds of excellent judges are the best he ever did. From time to time he published volumes of poetry, and with certain of his intimate friends he always maintained himself on the footing of a poet.

We remember the publication of his first volume, entitled "Ximena," which he never cared to reprint in his collected works. During his first European trip he wrote a great deal. Some of his shorter poems he afterwards published under the title "Rhymes of Travel." The fate of a longer poem we must hear in his own words.

"I had in my knapsack," he says, "a manuscript poem of some twelve hundred lines, called 'The Liberated Titan,'—the idea of which I fancied to be something entirely new in literature. Perhaps it was. I did not doubt for a moment that any London publisher would gladly accept it, and I imagined that its appearance would create not a little sensation. Mr. Murray gave the poem to his literary adviser, who kept it about a month, and then returned it with a polite message. I was advised to try Moxon; but, by this time, I had sobered down considerably, and did not wish to risk a second rejection.

"I therefore solaced myself by reading the immortal poem at night, in my bare chamber, looking occasionally down into the graveyard, and thinking of mute, inglorious Miltons.

"The curious reader may ask how I escaped the catastrophe of publishing the poem at last. That is a piece of good fortune for which I am indebted to the Rev. Dr. Bushnell, of Hartford. We were fellow-passengers on board the same ship to America, a few weeks later, and I had sufficient confidence in his taste to show him the poem. His verdict was charitable; but he asserted that no poem of that length should be given to the world before it had received the most thorough study and finish—and exacted from me a promise not to publish it within a year. At the end of that time I renewed the promise to myself for a thousand years."

Of other poems written at that time he thought better. In the preface to his volume he says of them,—"They are faithful records of my feelings at the time, often noted down hastily by the way-side, and aspiring to no higher place than the memory of some pilgrim who may, under like cir-cumstances, look upon the same scenes. An ivy leaf from a tower where a hero of old history may have dwelt, or the simplest weed growing over the dust that once held a great soul, is reverently kept for memories it inherited through the chance for-tune of the wind-sown seed; and I would fain hope that these rhymes may bear with them a like simple claim to reception, from those who have given me their company through the story of my wanderings."

Soon after he went to New York he began a series of Californian ballads, which were published anonymously in the *Literary World*, and attracted considerable attention. They appeared before he had made his trip to California; but while on that trip he wrote still others. At the same time he be-gan several more ambitious poems, among them "Hylas," and just before he set out for Egypt he had another volume of poems ready for the press. It was entitled "A Book of Romances, Lyrics and

Songs," and was published in Boston just after he set out on his Eastern journey. But while his volumes of travel sold edition after edition his volumes of verse scarcely paid expenses.

The previous year, however,—1850,—he had had a bit of success which caused him no end of annoyance. Jenny Lind had been brought to America to sing, and her manager had offered a prize of $200 for the best song that might be written for her. "Bayard Taylor came to me one afternoon early in September," says Mr. R. H. Stoddard, "and confided to me the fact that he was to be declared the winner of this perilous prize, and that he foresaw a row. 'They will say it was given to me because Putnam, who is my publisher, is one of the committee, and because Ripley, who is my associate on the *Tribune*, is another.'"

Mr. Stoddard kindly suggested to him that if he feared the results, he might substitute his (Stoddard's) name for the real one, and take the money while Stoddard got the abuse. He did not choose to do this, however, and the indignation of the seven or eight hundred disappointed contributors was unbounded. Taylor bore their abuse well enough, but he was heartily ashamed of the reputation which the poem brought him.

⟨

CHAPTER XI

"POEMS OF THE ORIENT"

During the months he spent in Egypt, Syria, and Asia Minor, Bayard Taylor wrote his "Poems of the Orient," of which Mr. Stoddard says, "I thought, and I think so still when I read these spirited and picturesque poems, that Bayard Taylor had captured the poetic secret of the East as no English-writing poet but Byron had. He knew the East as no one can possibly know it from books."

Certainly these poems of the East have a haunting ring that can never be forgotten. What more stirring than this Bedouin love song!

> From the desert I come to thee
> On a stallion shod with fire;
> And the winds are left behind

In the speed of my desire.
Under thy window I stand,
　And the midnight hears my cry:
I love thee, I love but thee,
　With a love that shall not die,
　　　Till the sun grows cold,
　　　And the stars are old,
　　　And the leaves of the Judgment
　　　　Book unfold!

Or what more grand and affectionate than this from '' Hassan to his Mare":

Come, my beauty! come, my desert darling!
　On my shoulder lay thy glossy head!
Fear not, though the barley-sack be empty,
　Here's the half of Hassan's scanty bread.

Thou shalt have thy share of dates, my beauty!
　And thou know'st my water-skin is free;
Drink and welcome, for the wells are distant,
　And my strength and safety lie in thee.

Bend thy forehead now, to take my kisses!
　Lift in love thy dark and splendid eye:
Thou art glad when Hassan mounts the saddle,—
　Thou art proud he owns thee: so am I.

Let the Sultan bring his boasted horses,
　Prancing with their diamond-studded reins;

They, my darling, shall not match thy fleetness
   When they course with thee the desert plains!

Let the Sultan bring his famous horses,
   Let him bring his golden swords to me,—
Bring his slaves, his eunuchs, and his harem;
   He would offer them in vain for thee.

We have seen Damascus, O my beauty!
   And the splendor of the Pashas there:
What's their pomp and riches?   Why, I would not
   Take them for a handful of thy hair!

Another stirring poem of the East is "Tyre."

The wild and windy morning is lit with lurid fire;
The thundering surf of ocean beats on the rocks of
   Tyre,—
Beats on the fallen columns and round the headlands'
   roars,
And hurls its foamy volume along the hollow shores,
And calls with hungry clamor, that speaks its long desire:
"Where are the ships of Tarshish, the mighty ships of
   Tyre?"

In his "L'Envoi" at the end of these poems,
Bayard Taylor gives us a hint of his meaning
when he spoke of his "southern nature" as distinguished from his "northern nature."

I found, among those Children of the Sun,
   The cipher of my nature,—the release
Of baffled powers, which else had never won
   That free fulfillment, whose reward is peace.

For not to any race or any clime
   Is the complete sphere of life revealed;
He who would make his own that round sublime,
   Must pitch his tent on many a distant field.

Upon his home a dawning lustre beams,
   But through the world he walks to open day,
Gathering from every land the prismal gleams,
   Which, when united, form the perfect ray.

CHAPTER XII

BAYARD TAYLOR'S FRIENDSHIPS

A biography of Bayard Taylor would not be complete without some account of his friendships. He was always on the best of terms with all living beings, and this subtle attraction of his nature was an important part of his greatness.

In "Views Afoot" he tells of a charming little incident which is enough in itself to make us love the man. It occurred in Florence, Italy, where he was a stranger, a foreigner; and this makes the incident in itself seem the more wonderful. "I know of nothing," he writes, "that has given me a more sweet and tender delight than the greeting of a little child, who, leaving his noisy playmates, ran across the street to me, and taking my hand, which he could barely clasp in both his soft little ones, looked up in my face with an expression so winning and affectionate that I loved him at once."

We recall the girl with the tea-cakes whom he met on his first journey while tramping across New Jersey. There was also something of human love and fellowship in his familiarity with wild animals in Egypt. In a free, joyous letter to his betrothed, Mary Agnew, he tells a curious incident of a similar kind, which occurred while he was editing the paper at Phœnixville. "On Sunday," says he, "I took [Schiller's] 'Don Carlos' with me in our boat, and rowed myself out of sight of the village into the solitude of the autumn woods. The sky was blue and bright as that of Eden, and the bright trees waved over me like gorgeous banners from the hilltops. I sat on a sunny slope and read for hours; it was a rare enjoyment! As I moved to rise I found a snake, which had crept up to me for warmth, and was coiled up quietly under my arm. I was somewhat startled, but the reptile slid noiselessly away, and I could not harm it."

A pretty story is told of Taylor by one who called on him when he was on one of his lecture tours. He was a stranger in the house of strangers, and no doubt as much a stranger to the cat as to any of the people; but it did not take him long to slip into easy intercourse with men or animals. "I had listened for some time to his intelligent descriptions, enunciated with extreme modesty in the modulated tones of his pleasing voice, when Tom, a large Maltese cat, entered the room. At Mr. Taylor's invitation Tom approached him, and as he stroked the fur of the handsome cat, a sort of magnetism seemed to be imparted to the family pet, for he rolled over at the feet of his new-made friend, and seemed delighted with the beginning of the interview. In the most natural manner possible, Mr. Taylor slid off, as it were, from the sofa on which he had been sitting, and assumed the position of a Turk on the rug before the sofa, playing with delighted Tom in the most buoyant manner, still continuing his conversation, but changing the subject, for the nonce, to that of cats, and narrating many stories respecting the weird and wise conduct of these animals, which are at once loved and feared by the human race."

He even felt a sort of personal tenderness for the old trees on his place at Kennett. He said that friends were telling him to cut this tree and cut that. To him this would have been almost a sacrilege. The trees seemed to depend on him for *protection*, and they should have it. Writing from this country home which he had built, he says, "The birds know me already, and I have learned to imitate the partridge and rain-dove, so that I can lure them to me."

And Bayard Taylor was the accepted friend of nearly all the distinguished men of letters of his time. He knew Longfellow, Lowell, Whittier, and Holmes in Boston, and even in his early years, when he first went to New York to work, he was able to pay them such flying visits as he describes in the following to Mary Agnew: "Reached Boston Sunday morning, galloped out to Cambridge, and spent the evening with Lowell; went on Monday to the pine woods of Abingdon to report Webster's speech, and dispatched it to the *Tribune;* got up early on Tuesday and galloped to Brookline to see Colonel Perkins; then off in the cars to Amesbury, and rambled over the Merrimac hills with Whittier; then Wednesday morning to Lynn, where I stopped a while at Helen Irving's; back in the afternoon to Cambridge, where I smoked a cigar with Lowell, and then stayed all night at Longfellow's."

In New York his enjoyment of his friends, whom he met often and familiarly, was of the keenest. Says Mr. R. H. Stoddard, "I recall many nights which Bayard Taylor spent in our rooms. . . . Great was our merriment; for if we did not always sink the shop, we kept it solely for our own amusement. Fitz-James O'Brien was a frequent guest, and an eager partaker of our merriment, which sometimes resolved itself into the writing of burlesque poems. We sat around a table, and whenever the whim seized us, we each wrote down themes on little pieces of paper, and putting them into a hat or box we drew out one at random, and then scribbled away for dear life. We put no restriction upon ourselves: we could be grave or gay, or idiotic even; but we must be rapid, for half the fun was in noting who first sang out, 'Finished!'"

The reader will remember Taylor's joy when a boy at receiving the autograph of Dickens. The time was coming when he should be on terms almost of intimacy with all the leading poets and writers of London. "I spent two days with Tennyson in June," he writes to a literary friend in 1857, "and you take my word for it, he is a noble fellow, every inch of him. He is as tall as I am, with a head which Read capitally calls that of a dilapidated Jove, long black hair, splendid dark eyes, and a full mustache and beard. The portraits don't look a bit like him; they are handsomer, perhaps, but haven't half the splendid character of his face. We smoked many a pipe together, and talked of poetry, religion, politics, and geology. . . . Our intercourse was most cordial and unrestrained, and he asked me, at parting, to be sure and visit him every time I came to England."

A similar tale might be told of his relations with Thackeray and a score of others.

But an account of his friendships would not be complete without a reference to Mr. Bufleb, whom he met on his journey up the Nile. Taylor writes to his mother from Nubia: "I want to speak of the friend from whom I have just parted, because I am very much moved by his kindness, and the knowledge may be grateful to you. His friendship for me is something wonderful, and it seems like a special Providence that in Egypt, where I anticipated the want of all near sympathy and kindness, I should find it in such abundant measure. He is a man of totally different experience from myself: accustomed all his life to wealth, to luxury, and to the exercise of authority. He was even prejudiced against America and the Americans, and he confessed to me that he was by nature stubborn and selfish. Yet few persons have ever placed such unbounded confidence in me, or treated me with such devotion and generosity. . . . For two days before our parting he could scarcely eat or sleep, and when the time drew near he was so pale and agitated that I almost feared to leave him. I have rarely been so moved as when I saw a strong, proud man exhibit such an attachment for me. . . . I told him all my history, and showed him the portrait I have with me [that of Mary Agnew]. He went out of the cabin after looking at it, and when he returned I saw that he had been weeping."

Surely, there must have been something peculiarly noble and sweet in Bayard Taylor's nature to have drawn to him so powerfully a man of another nation and another race. The friendship was lasting, and Taylor spent many happy weeks at Mr. Bufleb's home in Gotha, Germany. The latter even bought a little house and garden adjoining his own estate, which was for the special use of his friend, and he closes the letter which describes it by saying: "You see how I have written to you,

my dear Taylor.   In spite of our long separation
and remoteness from each other, your heart I
know could never tell you of any change in my
feelings and thoughts.   On the contrary, this
rapport which we enjoy has for me a profound
meaning; whilst you were dedicating your glorious
work on Central Africa to me, I was setting in
order for you the most cherished part of my
possessions."

CHAPTER XIII

LAST YEARS

With the building of Cedarcroft, and the publication of his "Poet's Journal," Bayard Taylor's
fame and fortune reached their height.   The Civil
War was now on the point of breaking out.   He
entered into the Northern cause with ardor, and
even sold a share of *Tribune* stock to raise a
thousand dollars with which to fit out his brother
Frederick and provide arms for his neighbors to
defend their homes.

But the war put an end to his lectures, and cut

off other sources of his income. In 1862 he was appointed secretary of legation at the court of St. Petersburg, and not long after was left there as *charge d'affaires.* The cause of the Union had received some heavy reverses, and France had invited England and Russia to join her in intervening between the combatants. But, perhaps owing to Bayard Taylor's diplomatic skill, Russia refused to take part in such an enterprise without the express desire of the United States.

About this time, also, Taylor began to write a series of novels, in the hope of bettering his fortunes thereby. The books brought him some reputation, but to-day "Hannah Thurston" and "John Godfrey's Fortunes" are seldom read.

A more important undertaking was his translation of "Faust," which was accepted abroad as a monument of his scholarship, and remains to-day one of the best translations into English of the great Goethe's most famous work.

Other books of travel were written and published, and various fresh volumes of poems. During this period of his life he produced most of his longer descriptive and philosophic poems, such as "The Picture of St. John," "Lars," and "Prince Deukalion"; but his songs and ballads have proved more popular than these, though he threw into them all his energy and ambition.

On July 4, 1876, he delivered his stately National Ode at the Philadelphia Centennial, and the same year he returned to his desk at the *Tribune* office. But failing health compelled him to give up this drudgery, and in the following year he was nominated United States minister to Berlin. A grand banquet at which Bryant presided was given him in New York, on April 4, the eve of his departure; but before the year was finished he died in Berlin —December 19, 1878.

NOTE.—The thanks of the publishers are due to Messrs. Houghton, Mifflin & Co. for permission to use extracts from "The Life and Poetical Works of Bayard Taylor."

www.ingramcontent.com/pod-product-compliance
Lightning Source LLC
Chambersburg PA
CBHW031428020726
47499CB00005B/1648